Dedicated to my mom and dad, who watched me spend hours writing and probably wondered why.

To sons Abraham and Elijah, who watched me spend hours writing and always believed in me.

To my wife Suzanne, who is beautiful in so many ways, and without whom, I would not be here today.

A Thriller So Abusive,
It's Criminal

KILLING THE BUTTERFLY

Dale Ward

Black Rose Writing | Texas

ISBN: 978-1-68433-951-8
PUBLISHED BY BLACK ROSE WRITING
www.blackrosewriting.com

Printed in the United States of America
Suggested Retail Price (SRP) $18.95

Killing the Butterfly is printed in Book Antiqua

*As a planet-friendly publisher, Black Rose Writing does its best to eliminate unnecessary waste to reduce paper usage and energy costs, while never compromising the reading experience. As a result, the final word count vs. page count may not meet common expectations.

KILLING THE BUTTERFLY

PART ONE

ONE

She moved in with her Aunt Meredith during the summer of her fourteenth year. And it had been fourteen years of chaos and madness. Especially the six months leading up to it all.

Sure, Aunt Meredith was nice and smart and friendly, and so Patty always wondered if she was indeed related. Her aunt's sister—her mother—had been so different: mean and stupid and unbearable. A new town, a new school (and high school at that), and so a new beginning. It made Patty excited, but anxious, and yes, somewhat terrified.

It's dark. The only light comes from a small lamp across the room. And the only light the lamp emits is a circle reflecting on the ceiling. Darkness is all around her. She is twelve years old. She is terrified. Her hands and feet are bound to the bed frame. Movement for her is impossible. She is naked on the bed—no sheet—no blanket. Exposed. Terrified. Cold. Hurting. Crying. Alone.

With a burst of energy—brought on by terror—she arches her back. Again and again. It's all she can do. The small of her back rises only inches, then back down again. The bed bounces a little, but the bindings hold. The bouncing bed—vibrating—shaking—loosens the bulb in the lamp, and the light is extinguished. The circle of light on the ceiling disappears. Leaving darkness. Total darkness. Even though she can see nothing, she closes her eyes tight. And cries.

Later. She is aware of another presence. She knows it is still pitch black in the room, even though she keeps her eyes shut tight. Her binds are still holding as she feels his weight on her and feels his breath on her cheek. Darkness—like a cave. She smells sweat. Not hers.

She cries and cries and cries. Her twelve-year-old mind doesn't understand. She is confused. Lost. Alone. Darkness. And tears.

For two years she had these nightmares—or to her, visions, because they were so vivid and intense. These visions hidden away in a secret compartment of her mind. Buried. They never came to light until a new vision emerged. It was then she remembered the others. After the fifth vision, something clicked, and they began to haunt her waking hours. Even though she wanted to tell someone, there was no one for her to confide in. She had no friends. No family of worth. And she trusted no one. So the visions remained hidden from the world.

The first part of her fourteenth year—her last days in middle school—had been a mess. Not surprising, they called her into the counselors' offices. Dr. Alice, the school counselor, was friendly enough, but sort of scary at the same time.

"Hello, Patty," Dr. Alice said, shutting the door behind her.

That afternoon in particular, Patty was feeling the desolation of her empty life. All alone, and the visions were weighing her down. The nightmares. Her shoulders hunched and her back was bent under the burden of the heavy darkness. Her dirty blond hair, cut to the shoulders, hung down around her face. Patty sat in a brown leather chair facing the desk. Dr. Alice was on the other side in a wingback chair—black—behind her a bookcase overflowed with books bearing titles such as "Stay Smart," "Finding the Real You," "This Is a Circus," and other such stuff. She had a photograph that showed what must have been her family, including herself, a middle-aged man, and two kids—one girl and one boy. The perfect little clan. What did she really know about dysfunction? What did she really know about horror and monsters?

Dr. Alice twiddled her pen. It looked like a really fancy pen. Patty picked at her thumbnail. The counselor just sat and stared. Silence. With those eyes looking through her. This is a girl who does not understand how pretty she is—or could be, if she cared at all. Smallish and thin, with perfect skin and complexion. But she only stared down into her lap, her face covered by her hair and in silence.

Patty could not look back—still interested in her thumbnail.

Finally, the counselor. "How has school been for you these past several weeks?"

Patty shrugged. "Okay." What all did Dr. Alice know?

"Have you made many friends?"

No. She shrugged. None.

Dr. Alice jotted, then said, "Can you share with me anything about your mother? It's been several weeks, and for you to be healthy, you need to talk to someone. That's why I'm here, you know. Do you miss her? Have you been crying a lot?"

She hasn't shed a tear for her mom. Patty stared at Dr. Alice for a second, deciding what—if anything—she wanted to say. Finally—what the hell...

⚫ ⚫ ⚫

Mother the Witch. God Rest Her Soul, indeed.

Patty remembered the last thing she had ever said to Mother the Witch: *You Suck!* She remembered since that was about the only thing she ever said to her mother to begin with. Patty was forced to live with her, no other place to go—her dad sure didn't want her anymore. She had stayed with him on and off since the divorce, but his favorite pastime was the bottle. And so she was stuck with mommy. The worst part was she had to live not only with Mother, but with her evil step-clan—sharing a room with Brat Erin.

"Don't touch my stuff," Erin said. "It's mine."

Like Patty would want any of her trendy crap. Erin had a couple of posters of the latest loser boy toy singer hanging on the wall above her bed. And then hearts and flower crap—stickers and what-not—glued around the posters. More flowers on her bedspread, and then a ton of stupid stuffed animals for her to practice her hugging and kissing on. Ridiculous.

One night—alone in the room—Patty snuck a peek at her diary—just to see what kind of tripe stuff she was getting into. Cute Boy this, Cute Boy that, that was about it. And then Erin walked in on her.

"Get out of my journal!"

"What you got to hide?" Patty asked, as Erin yanked the book out of her hands.

"It's none of your damn business!" Erin grabbed Patty's folder of poems and flung it across the room. All the papers came flying out of it and landed everywhere. "How do you like it!" Erin yelled.

Patty jumped up and tackled her, scratching and clawing at her any way she could. Erin fought back—screaming—and they rolled around on the floor. A lamp fell over. The desk chair went down. She grabbed Patty's hair, pulling hard, and Patty yelled.

"You little brat!" Patty yelled. And she actually punched Erin in the mouth.

It was Erin's turn to scream as Mother the Witch pulled Patty off of her. "What are you doing, Patty! Get off of her!"

"She started it," Patty said.

Mother threw Patty across the room and she landed on the floor by the bed. "Don't you move," she said, pointing her bony finger at her. She helped Erin sit up, who was crying, holding onto her mouth. Patty saw a little blood, and it made her feel good.

"Let me see, sweetheart." Mother pulled her hand away and Patty could see Erin had a fat lip. Ha! "Oh, honey, let's put some ice on that." She helped Erin up and glared at Patty. "You are grounded, young lady. And I don't know for how long."

Oh, did she mean she and her evil step-clan would leave her alone? That's great, Patty thought, but instead she said to her, "You suck!"

Mother slammed the door on her way out.

After the icing down, Mother the Witch and Deadbeat Joe took Brat Erin and brother Bart Fart to Gooey's Pizza, since Erin was suffering from so much trauma. Patty thought, *Give me a break*. They had left her in the bedroom—door closed—but she ventured out soon after she heard the car leaving the driveway, thunder rolling in the distance.

Yeah—no sign of them. You'd know it right away because Deadbeat Joe was never anywhere else but in the big chair directly in front of the television. On days when he worked, you'd find the chair vacant, but he only worked a couple of days a week. So for much of the time, there he'd sit. And son Bart Fart was not much better. He did nothing around the house except give Patty shit whenever he had the chance. A big fat bully—worthless in her eyes.

They were gone for the longest time. At ten o'clock, Patty wondered if they were ever coming home. But she knew she couldn't be so lucky. *Be careful what you wish for*, she thought, because the doorbell rang about eleven-fifteen. Outside stood a police officer.

"Do you know Joyce Monroe and Joseph Valdez?" he said, and Patty nodded. "They have two children: Bartholomew Valdez and a daughter." She nodded again, and all of time slowed down.

"Joyce is my mother. The others are step family."

"There's been a horrible accident."

· · ·

None of them survived. It had been raining, and the roads were slick. On the way home from Gooey's, while on the interstate, they skidded out of control and slammed into a concrete barrier. The car flipped, landed on its roof, and then slid down an embankment and into Willow River.

Patty didn't shed a tear at the funeral. Mother had no friends of her own outside of the Joe sphere, so all the people who came were strangers to Patty. Except Aunt Meredith. Aunt Meredith shed a lot of tears — but then she hadn't lived with Mother for a long time.

Dad actually showed up. He was looking fairly healthy, which meant sober. He told Patty he had been dry for sixth months. Patty guessed that was good, but as far as her immediate future, she had little choice. Since she had stayed with Dad periodically throughout the years, she moved in with Dad after the funeral: the middle of March of her fourteenth year.

· · ·

Dr. Alice jotting again. "That's a lot for anyone to experience, much less a fourteen-year-old." Silence. "Your grades seem to holding up pretty well. That's good."

"I don't have much else to do."

"Do you have any hobbies?"

"Laundry. Cooking for two." She paused. Dare she share anything personal? "I like to write. Mostly poetry. And sometimes I like to imagine I am in romantic far-away places and write essays about them — travel pieces."

"Those are great outlets. And it looks like you have top grades in your language arts classes. So your teachers must think you are an excellent writer. I'd love to read some of your stuff if I may."

Patty shrugged again.

"Can we meet again? Same time Friday? And will you bring in some of your writings?"

"I guess. Can I go now?"

Again dark. Again immobile. The lamp now relit, but still dim, and far, far away. Her hands are tied together above her head. There is no slack. Her right ankle, tied to the far corner, creates a silhouette of her foot by the light of the lamp. Her left leg disappears off toward the far left corner. It, too, tied tight. She is clad in only a t-shirt, scrunched up around her chest. Nothing else on. She is sore, and fading in and out. Then she hears a crash — a bottle perhaps — outside the room — far away. Followed by the sound of a masculine voice — short, quick, angry.

Patty can only look straight up toward the ceiling. The tears start. Each eye producing a salty river down the sides of her face, over her temples, around each ear. Her body shakes. She is terrified. Thirteen — or any age — is too young to be in a place like this. No one should be in a place like this.

Friday. Back in Dr. Alice's office. She is reading the poems Patty brought in. She brought in some gloomy ones. And one of her favorites about the Butterfly. And then a travel piece on her imagined visit to an out island in the Bahamas — remote and quiet.

"I see why your teachers give you good grades. These are superb. A bit dark, perhaps, but good." Dr. Alice made yet another note. "Why so dark?"

A new fingernail inspection by Patty.

"What is bothering you? You can talk to me. Nothing you say leaves this room, and it can only help. Don't you want someone to talk to?"

"It's stupid."

"Nothing is stupid, Patty. Tell me about it."

"Mainly bad dreams. They're dark all right."

"What sort of dreams?"

Another shrug. "It's dark. It's cold. I can't move."

"Why can't you move?"

"I'm tied up." A pause. "And I'm naked."

Momentary silence filled the air. Patty heard Dr. Alice's pen on the paper.

"Then what happens?" Dr. Alice waited for a reply.

"The monster comes in. I scream. I cry." Patty felt a tear from each eye run down her cheeks. She quickly wiped them off with the back of her hand. "Then it's later and I wake up." A sniffle. "It's frightening," she said. "I come to—terrified. Like I was actually there."

Dr. Alice jotted again on her notepad with her fancy pen. Looked at Patty. "Do you know this place?"

Patty shook her head. "It's so dark—I can't make anything out. And I'm tied down so I can't look around too well."

"Have you told anybody else about these?"

"No. There's no one for me to talk to. I don't have any friends. I'm all alone."

"You should try to find a friend, Patty."

"I'm too weird. Too quiet. Everyone treats me like I don't exist. I'm invisible."

Dr. Alice put her pen down and sat back in her big chair. She clasped her hands together in her lap. "I'm sure there are others out there who are quiet-types, too. Maybe if you just tried talking to them. They may become friends."

Patty frowned. What did this have to do with anything? Maybe she was wasting her time here. Why did she say anything? She thought they were talking about her weird dreams and now Dr. Alice wants her to make friends.

"I've tried. It never works. Besides, it's better to be invisible. That way, no one gives me trouble. They just leave me alone."

"I see." Dr. Alice sat back up and picked up her pen. She jotted some more. "Where's your father?"

In response, Patty looked around for a clock. Saw none. "What time is it? Mid-afternoon? He's probably drunk in some bar by now. He treats me like I don't exist, too. Invisible." Silence again. Nothing— from the doctor or Patty. Patty now noticed the clock behind her making sounds — tick tock, tick tock. Dr. Alice could keep track of time, but Patty couldn't.

Finally, Dr. Alice closed her notebook and folded her hands. "Dreams of darkness and immobility. I think the darkness means your outlook is dreary. I think being tied up means you think you cannot change your circumstance." She gave her a quick smile. "But you can, Patty. You have options. You have choices."

"Like what?" Patty crossed her arms across her chest and slumped back in the chair.

"Well, let's try this: come back and see me next week. Between now and then, I want you to talk to at least three people. Ask them about themselves: what music do they like? Movies? Books? Find something you have in common and talk about it with them. Next week we'll talk about how it went." She smiled again. Patty didn't particularly like her smile. "Can we try this?"

Patty shrugged.

"The world can be a lot less dark with someone else to share it with."

Quiet again.

"OK?" she asked.

Patty got up and grabbed her bag. She suddenly wanted to be out of there. "Sure," she said on her way out the door.

Seeking the warmth Seeking the sun
Flying south and always on the run
You can't catch what doesn't stop
The butterfly — perpetually in flight

Patty sat again with Dr. Alice. It was the following week. She didn't know why she had brought up the dreams. The admission had come from Patty in a rush of words and emotions. But she had had another dream last night and told her so. Again, the counselor made no comment about this last memory/vison/dream/nightmare. Her jotting in her notebook was the only initial reaction.

Finally, she looked up. "You heard a voice this time?"

"Yes. And no, I couldn't recognize it. It was low. Raspy and deep. Could have been the monster."

Patty wiped a lone tear that had leaked from her left eye.

"I'm sorry," Dr. Alice said. "These are horrible memories. No one should have to endure something like this—real or imagined."

"You think I am making this up?"

"No no no! Absolutely not! These are real to you. But even you call them dreams or visions or nightmares—as real as these may be. Horrible. Disturbing. Not made up." Dr. Alice did not sound too convincing to Patty, and she quickly changed the subject. "Patty, were you able to talk to people this week? I have noted here you were to talk to three people."

Patty shrugged. "Talked to two people. It didn't really go too well, so I didn't bother a third time. Three strikes, you know."

Dr. Alice fixed her hands in front of her. "Can you tell me about it? Whom did you first approach?"

"Kailee. I said, 'Hi.' She said, 'Hi.' She said, 'What do you want?' I said, 'Nothing,' which is what she wanted from me: nothing."

"I don't know if that was a very good attempt. What happened with the second person?"

"Carleigh. She's kind of retro-goth. I asked her about the shirt she had on: Azor Swan. She's some singer. I'd heard about her before and she sounded interesting. Carleigh proceeded to tell me how she saw Azor Swan at her last concert stop a couple of weeks ago. Carleigh said she was so embarrassed because she had to take her mom along. Then she started trashing her mom like she was some piece of shit, but she sounded OK to me. My mom would have slashed her wrists before she would have gone to a concert with me."

"Did you tell Carleigh that?"

"No—I just told her my mother was dead. She stopped talking after that and said she had to go. See—my mother still haunts me and screws things up. Mommy the Bitch—God rest her soul."

TWO

Patty had moved in with her father after the funeral. She had hoped to go it alone, but social services, the school, even dad wouldn't have it. She got four days and nights on her own in mom and Joe's place, and then the house was on the market and she found herself at dad's. Turn the page. New chapter. Life just carries on.

She had stayed at her dad's every once in a while after he and the witch divorced. That was three years ago. The one condition was that he had to be sober for Patty to stay at his place. That was his rule as much as Patty's. She guessed neither one of them—or mom for that matter—liked it when he was on a bender. He'd drink for days, usually lose a job, sometimes end up in the hospital (or jail), and then dry out again for several weeks (months? days?). Whatever.

"I got six-month sobriety, Patty," he told her proudly when she was first given the option of moving in with him. Pretty much the only option other than juvenile—or foster—no thank you. Lesser of three evils, she guessed. "And I'm done with the bottle," he added. Of course, she had all heard that before.

He had a small, two-bedroom house, one bath, a small kitchen, living room, and a dining room. It had a basement, but who knew what all lived down there. Not Patty, for sure. She got one of the bedrooms. It was about eight feet by six feet—enough for a mattress and then a small dresser. There was a closet with a sliding door. Not much, but it was all hers. Her earthly possessions were minimal: mainly jeans, shirts, boots/shoes, some travel books/magazines, and then her journals. She liked to write poetry, so she spent her spare time with her music in her ears (courtesy of her phone and her earbuds), and her nose in her poetry—or a book. Most of the books were travel or geography, or she'd read the travel magazines. It seems most people hope of things unattainable, right? She'd never get to visit these exotic locations and foreign countries, beaches and mountains, so she might as well daydream about them. She didn't know if she could pinpoint one favorite location, but she had several that stayed on the top of her list: Tahiti, Aruba, Panama maybe, Paris, of course. Tokyo would be fascinating. Dream dream away. She was stuck in Missouri. How exotic is that?

Dad's house was further from school than mom's had been, so Patty was spending more time on buses. Bouncing around—hard to write—noisy—with a lot of kids of all ages. She tried to sit up front. It was less bouncy, and sitting by the driver (Lakeisha), kept other kids from coming up and bothering her. And Lakeisha always had music on. Patty developed a real taste for Lakeisha-type music. She'd get home after school about the same time that dad got home from work. He'd bring dinner home some nights. A veritable smorgasbord of burgers one night, tacos another, sometimes chicken, other times something like chili or spaghetti for Patty to cook up, which she did. Figured she could do her part.

The TV would come on—whatever sport was in season, and dad would plant in front of it until he fell asleep in his chair. Patty stayed in her room after dinner. Didn't want to crimp his lifestyle. He'd been alone for so long, it was probably an adjustment for him to have a fourteen-year-old girl suddenly hanging around. They tried to talk at dinner, but it was usually pretty banal.

"How was school?"

"Fine."

"You got any homework?"

"A little. I got some math. You want to help me?"

"No. I wouldn't be any help."

"How was your day?"

"Fine. I put brakes on a Nissan."

That was about it. Then he'd move to his chair so he could watch the game. And she'd move to her room—music and books, sometimes a night of videos on her phone of beaches and exotic locales far, far away...

The butterfly fluttered
Caught in the web
The more it moved, the deeper it bled.
The spider, not hurried
Licked its lips
Mandibles at the ready

"I am so sorry. I should have picked up on the signs." This was Dr. Alice talking. Patty had gone to see her—was told she had to go see her—although she would have anyway—after the incident. "I feel horrible. Please forgive me."

Patty just looked at her. Sitting silent.

"You don't have to talk about it, but it might help you." She paused. "It might help me help you."

Patty took a deep breath. She might as well tell her the details. She probably knew them all anyway.

Patty had been stupid to trust again in a sobriety that never lasted. Never had, never will, and will she ever learn? But the Monster had been sober for six months, so she moved in with him. Stupid girl.

All was well for three weeks—right up near the end of eighth grade. She cooked for him. Cleaned for him. Did his laundry. And somehow, graduation was a week away.

But then it happened. It was a Friday. A beautiful day, actually. The windows were open, and a breeze cooled the house. Patty was heating a pot of bean soup for the two of them. He had mentioned taking her to a movie that night. Of course, it had to be a loud, explosive action pic, but better than sitting in his little two-bedroom house and watching baseball or boxing or some stupid survivalist show. Dad usually got home about five thirty from his latest job—this go-around as an auto mechanic. When it got to be five forty-five, Patty considered maybe traffic was bad. When it got to be six, she thought he might have stopped off for a drink or two (or six).

At seven, the Monster stumbled in the door. Patty was doing her dishes; his dishes still on the table. He set his lunch pail on the little table by the door, and set his "coffee" mug next to it, splashing whatever he had in it on his hand. He brought his hand to his mouth to lick it dry, and then he noticed her.

"Oh, hey Missy," he said. "I forgot you were here." He came further into the kitchen, and then over to her at the sink. "Come here, missy, give me a hug."

Patty became a statue—not moving an inch—staring straight ahead and not at him. "Leave me alone, dad."

"Is that any way to welcome your dad home from work—slaving all day so you can sit here, do nothing, and eat my food?"

He came over behind her and tried to turn her around. "Come on. Turn around and give me a hug." She grabbed the edge of the counter—one hand on each side of her—and held on tight. Dad tried to turn her around by her shoulders.

"Leave me alone, dad!"

"I just want to be friendly! Come on!"

For a moment, all was quiet. He paused, but his backhand was fast. And it hurt as it hit the side of her face. It also knocked her over onto the floor.

He stumbled to the floor, too, off balance, and Patty jumped on his back and began to pound as hard as she could on the back of his head. She didn't think it was very hard, though. Not hard enough.

Dad smirked a little and stood up. Patty was holding on and still trying to hit him—riding around on his back. "I'll give you a piggyback ride, missy."

She screamed now, as he twisted, now able to grab her. But she was kicking, yelling, clawing, screaming—doing anything to get away from him—but his hold was secure as he took her into his bedroom and slammed the door behind him. More screaming and yelling. Patty fighting as hard as she could. He was strong, slurring his words, yelling as loud as she was screaming. They bounced off the furniture, knocked over a lamp. Her shirt torn, shoulder bared, and then he lost his balance. He fell over. A crash as his head hit the corner of the table. A thud. And then silence.

In such a short time, a room could really get trashed. The table was overturned, and the lamp, now familiar, was lying on the floor—the shade somewhat crumpled and the bulb smashed. The comforter pulled halfway off the bed. She sat on the floor next to the bed. Her breathing was heavy. Her face in her hands, making little noises — trying to keep from crying. The Monster was lying on the floor — kind of half on his side and half on his back — his eyes were closed and he was next to the overturned nightstand. There was a pool of blood forming at the back of his head. Patty wondered if he was dead. Hoping he was.

•

The neighbors had heard the ruckus and had called the police. Patty was glad, because she didn't know if she would have been able to. It was obvious to the police what had happened. Patty had fixed her shirt as best as she could. She told them this was not the first time. She couldn't remember how many times. Which might have meant five or could have meant fifty. All she knew was that he was ugly. He was The Monster.

The police hauled him away. He wasn't dead. He was hurting, and his head damaged. But nowhere near the damage he had caused her.

It was Dr. Alice who actually suggested Patty move in with Aunt Meredith. And after Aunt Meredith accepted, she was ecstatic.

"A new start!" she said. "New location. New city. New school. You can make new friends — I mean you should make new friends. You *will* make new friends! Promise me you will make at least one new friend."

Patty nodded.

"Excellent. Of course, you can still come see me." That was not likely. Too far away. "You can call me if nothing else."

Patty almost got the feeling that Dr. Alice was excited not only for her moving on, but for the fact she *was* moving on. She would be rid of her. Patty knew she was an exceptional case, a most difficult one. She guessed some shrinks would be excited about the challenge, but Dr. Alice seemed intimidated.

Patty broke it off clean. "Good bye, doctor. Thanks for the help." And she knew she'd never see or hear from her again.

THREE

The butterfly – in flight
Cannot fight the pull of the light
The closer she gets (she has learned)
The more she'll get burned

Patty moved in with her Aunt Meredith the summer before she became a high school freshman. Things went pretty well that summer, so she stayed on with Aunt Meredith and enrolled in Jefferson High School. Patty knew no one in school, and that first day, her first class was Biology. They hook you up with another student – a lab partner – and she was told her partner was a junior – the only junior in the class (most students took Biology as a freshman) – but her partner – a boy, to make matters worse – wasn't there when class started. Just great.

The teacher, Mr. Yaeger, wanted everyone to get to know their lab partner right away, so he assigned a leaf to each couple to decipher what kind of tree it came from – using the genus key he handed out. Moving through all the questions on the key (and marking the right answers) would lead the students to the type of tree for their particular leaf.

The room immediately got noisy as lab partners started talking and laughing and decoding, but Patty quietly started on hers alone.

Mr. Yaeger appeared over my shoulder. "Patty, your lab partner is notorious for being late, I'm afraid. That is when he bothers to show up for school."

She nodded.

"Being the first day of school and all," he continued, "I thought maybe—just maybe—he'd show up and be on time. But no. He gets his first tardy of the year—one for one, so far."

Just then, the classroom door crashed open and Patty and Mr. Yaeger both looked up. In walked this rough-looking, but extremely good-looking guy—almost pretty if he had made an effort. But messed up hair and grungy jeans. There he stood, his eyes moving around the room, a smirk on his face.

Mr. Yaeger waved him over. "Well, there he is now," he said. "Roy, over here, please."

The smirk grew to a smile (gorgeous), and he ambled over.

It was only eight thirty-five, but Mr. Yaeger said, "Good afternoon, Roy."

"Ha! Good one, Mr. Yaeger. Sorry I'm late. My car wouldn't start."

"I see." Mr. Yaeger indicated Patty, and she looked away for a second. "This is Patty. She's your lab partner for the year."

She looked at Roy, and he tilted his head. "I ain't seen you around before," he said.

"She is new to our school district," Mr. Yaeger said. "Make her feel welcomed and at home, and help her figure out the genus of the leaf, please." Mr. Yaeger moved off, and Roy sat down.

"Hello, Patty." He leaned in close to her and she caught a whiff of his scent—not deodorized, but not awful, either. "What you got there?"

"We are supposed to find out what kind of tree this leaf comes from."

"Ha! Big tall one," he said, and then that smile. "It's an elm."

"Well, we're supposed to use this key to figure it out."

"That's stupid. It's an elm. Done!"

Patty shook the key twice. "I don't think that's the point," she said.

"Yeah, stupid is the point." He wrote down "elm" on their sheet. "Done." And then he leaned back in his chair. She felt his eyes on her, traveling down and then back up again. "Ah, you're a blusher, huh?" Which only made her blush more. "Kind of cute, too." This guy was impossible. "Want to do something after school?"

She frowned. "No—I just met you not even five minutes ago."

"Ah—worried I'm a psycho killer. No worries—I am." And then he laughed.

Her class schedule was sitting on the top of her notebook pile (stupid girl), and he grabbed it.

"Let's see," he said. "Aw—we do not have any other classes together. Sixth hour you have American History, Room 242. I'll be waiting for you after class."

6th hour let out with the ringing of the bell. Patty didn't think she was watching the clock any more than usual, but it felt like it a little. By the time the last echo of the bell had rung, all the kids had stampeded out the doors. Patty held up the rear. She did not know anyone, had no friends (Dr. Alice immediately came to her mind), and had nowhere to go except to her aunt's place. No hurry here.

Mrs. Barton, the American History teacher, was wiping down her board. She noticed Patty leaving, and she looked over her shoulder.

"Have a good evening, Patty. It's nice to have you in our school."

"Bye," she said. Mrs. Barton seemed nice.

Patty stepped out into the hallway. It was empty. Not that she expected him to be standing there or anything, but she did look around in all directions. No such Roy. Oh well. He seemed a little rough around the edges, anyway. A bad boy, for sure. Was that the attraction? Looking for her father in all the wrong places?

As she rounded the corner, he jumped out.

"HA!"

Her books fell to the floor.

He laughed.

She exhaled slowly. "You are not funny."

"Yeah, kind of funny," he said, bending over to pick up the notebooks. "I saw you looking around for me."

"I was not."

"You were. No doubt about it."

"Look. I'm new here. I'm was trying to get my bearing."

Roy handed her the notebooks. "OK, sure." She knew he didn't believe her. "Let me give you a ride home."

"No."

As they walked down the hall. Out the door to the parking lot.

"I got a classic. They don't make 'em like this anymore."

She assumed he was talking about the beat up, old compact, held together by good luck and duct tape.

"I'm not getting in that," she said.

Roy stepped in front of her and faced her squarely. "Look. We get in. I won't bite. I'll take you to Super Shop. You can get a foo-foo coffee or a freeze, soda, whatever the hell you want. And then I'll take you home."

Oh, so confident. It's why she got in.

Two eagles and a rabbit
The rabbit on the run
Knows it won't last
The rabbit gets away
To see another day
As the two eagles clash

The next day, after 6th hour, Roy was nowhere to be found. Patty figured he'd jump out at her from behind the corner, but he wasn't there. Oh well.

She had made her way down the hallway. It was pretty much deserted. It was amazing how quickly the halls could empty at the last bell of the day. A guy named Bob was at the drinking fountain. He stood up and wiped his mouth as she passed. "Hi," he said. "You're Patty, right?"

"That's right," she said, as he fell in step with her.

"I'm Bob."

"Hi, Bob."

"We have Geometry together."

"Yeah, that's right."

"Oh, you noticed, huh? I just thought you were the new quiet girl who sat in the corner."

"Yeah, that's right."

He laughed at her. They walked down the steps together.

"You like your new school?"

Patty shrugged.

"Wow," he said. "That much, huh?"

She shrugged again. Another girl went running past them and out the door. She said, "Hi, Bob," on the way out. Bob held the door for Patty.

"Thanks," she said.

"Yeah, I'm a real gentleman."

A horn honked as they stepped into the sunlight, and she saw Roy. He waved at her from inside his car.

"Oh, it looks like you already have a ride," Bob said before she could say anything. Before she could even confirm or deny it. Before she could confirm in her mind that she was going home with Roy. Now she seemed committed to it. "Well, Patty, it was nice talking to you." Bob headed off to the left. Just like that. She walked over to Roy.

"Hello, Patty," Roy said. He opened the passenger side door for her. She hesitated, but got in. Roy looked angry. He slammed her door and then got in behind the wheel. "What are you talking to that dill wad for?" he asked.

"He was just being friendly."

Roy actually looked very mad. "Well, I don't like it." He jumped back out of the car, saying, "I'll be right back. Don't move."

His door slammed, and he jogged off toward where Bob was turning the corner around the History building. Roy disappeared around the building, too.

Hmm. She sat and waited. A minute turned into a couple, and she was just about to get out, when Roy reappeared. He came jogging back and jumped in. He was huffing and puffing, and she could tell he was all fired up.

"He won't bother you no more," Roy said.

"Roy, he wasn't bothering me."

Roy grabbed her chin and pulled her towards him. His face got close to hers, and she could see it was flushed. "I don't want you talking to other guys. Got it?"

Patty started to complain, but decided against it. Instead, she just nodded as best she could through the tight grip he held on her chin.

Then he released her and started the car.

"Good," he said. "Glad that's settled."

They drove off, and she noticed his knuckles on the steering wheel. They looked very red, and one of them had a slight cut on it.

FOUR

Roy was hurrying to heat the chili he had made for himself and his father. The old bastard had just pulled up outside, as evidenced by the loud muffler—or lack of such—on his truck. Roy never knew what time his old man would get home. It all depended on how the money held out at the bar. Could be six. Could be midnight. Tonight it was eight, so he could count on his dad being primed up and ready to be a prick. The earlier times meant he might not be too lit up yet, and the late time usually meant passing out immediately in bed. If the old man wasn't home by ten, Roy would eat alone.

The door crashed open.

"Well, if it ain't the little shit," his old man bellowed. "What you got there? Something to eat?"

"Chili."

"Good, I'm starving." He crashed down into his chair at the table. Roy's dad sat in the same chair for every meal. He could see the TV from there, if it was on, and he was so inclined to watch it. Tonight, he just sat there and scratched his unshaven face. He had quite a bit of growth, not having shaved in more than three days. Fairly common, that was—not shaving often. If he shaved, it was on Friday nights, especially if he was "going out," which only meant a different bar than the one he usually stopped off at after work.

Roy slopped some chili into a couple of bowls and brought them to the table. One table with two chairs in a small kitchen. No room for much else. The chairs were wooden, as was the table, vintage 1940 probably. These were not purchased as an antique item, but were purchased because that was what was available at the garage sale. The kitchen cabinets were small: two hanging, and one on each side of the sink. Above the sink, an old-style clock with minute and hour hands—hands actually pointing with an index finger. The second hand—red and thin—moved in its circular path, everything working together silently telling its tale of time: 7 minutes and 23 seconds past the hour of eight. An old refrigerator, this was vintage mid-1990's, sat next to the back door.

"We got any beer in the fridge?"

Roy knew to always have beer in the fridge, and at seventeen, he had always found creative ways to stock it: usually stealing it in some fashion or another. He popped two cans and added these to the dinner. His old man didn't give a shit if Roy drank. He didn't give a shit pretty much about anything when it came to Roy.

The old man slurped down some beer, then shoved a mouthful of chili into his mouth. He immediately spat it out. And he backhanded Roy on the side of the face.

"Son of a bitch! You trying to burn the hell out of my mouth, kid?"

Roy held his cheek. His eyes moistened as they glared. "Maybe you should blow on it first?"

His dad jumped up and knocked Roy backwards in his chair. Roy's head slammed onto the floor.

"I take no lip from you, son!"

His dad picked up Roy's bowl of chili and dumped it onto Roy's face. "Blow on this!" his dad said.

Roy rolled over and grabbed his face. It was burning. The old man grabbed the back of Roy's neck and shoved his face into the bean mess on the linoleum floor.

"You give me respect, boy!" as he held Roy's face down. Then he released him. "Now clean this shit up!" his dad growled. "I'm going to bed." And he stumbled out of the kitchen.

Roy stayed on the floor. Fuming.

. . .

Roy's school attendance was atrocious. Tardies. Absences. He covered them all. The reasons varied—some better than others: sickness, hangover, tired, black eye, busted lip. When he was there, he rarely spoke, rarely did his school work, or never made any friends. One such day, when Roy decided to award the school with his presence, the remains of a black eye and a busted lip were still slightly visible — more than he had figured anyway — because someone noticed. Even made a comment.

"Hey, Roy! Your mom beat you up again?" This came from Austin Guthrie, having a moment of stupidity. He got the laughs from the group of kids standing around him — which was the reaction he was after. He did not plan on the next reaction.

Roy's eyes flashed. Immediate rage — although he kept it inside fairly well — temporarily. Roy grabbed Austin by the front of his shirt. Austin's eyes went wide. The group of kids all took a step back. They were in a corner of the lunchroom, and, off to the side, was a storage closet. Roy shoved Austin toward the closet — still holding on — opened the door — and threw Austin inside. He crashed into a mop bucket and fell to the floor. Roy snapped on the light and let the door close quietly.

Anger management had always been an issue for Roy, especially when it came to his father's treatment of him, and even more so, his deceased mother — which tied into his father's mistreatment of those around him. His release of this anger onto poor Austin was swift and effective. The well placed kick to the ribs would remain painful and well hidden. A second kick was equally effective. But Roy was wanting to make an example of Austin. He wanted the example to scream the warning: *Do not talk about my mother or else you should expect bruises!*

Grasping Austin again by his shirt front, Roy pulled him off the floor — the pain in Austin's ribs evident by the tears in his eyes and the grimace on his face. But no compassion from Roy. The first punch landed on Austin's left eyebrow. The second on his top lip. And the third on his nose. Blood poured from all three locations. With the next couple of punches, Roy had made some sick game — although unconsciously and not deliberate — to see if he could hit Austin hard enough with his right hand to knock him free from the hold with his left hand — but no, Roy could hold him securely off the ground by his shirt front. One more punch to the same eye for good measure, then Roy let Austin drop back to the floor.

When Roy came out of the closet, the group was still assembled outside, some with their mouths open, all extremely quiet. In fact, the whole lunchroom was still, and they focused all eyes on Roy. He stopped for a moment and returned the gazes—looking slowly from one side of the room to the other. He hadn't noticed the several blood splotches and splashes on his shirt, but everyone else did.

Roy turned and left the building.

• • •

The day after, Roy had taken the highway to the neighboring town. On days he skipped school, he found it easier if he got away from the hometown to hang out. No hassles from the local Jefferson cops—who knew him by now—or other parents—who also knew him—and they'd all make comments—or worse yet—as far as the cops were concerned—haul him back to school. Very embarrassing and not the making of a good day.

In the next town over, Roy was a stranger. He could park his old junker and wander around. No one seemed to care. Always with an eye out for a new car, Roy found himself in the parking lot of the big factory in town: Parker's Springs. There was a guard shack, but it was really far away at the other side on the corner of the parking lot, and since he was on foot, he easily jumped the fence and got inside unnoticed.

Roy moved through the cars, looking for either an unlocked car with free treasures inside, or a car with something noticeably worth breaking into. It would have to be something worth the trouble and risk of breaking a window—a gun, for instance—like someone would be stupid enough to leave one in sight—but you never know.

At the edge of the parking lot—away from both the factory and the guard shack, Roy discovered an unlocked car. It was a small compact, fairly beat up, with no special treasures inside other than a thrash metal CD, but when he opened the door, he heard the ding-ding-ding sound. No way, Roy thought, but sure enough, the keys dangled from the ignition. Who could be so stupid? Their loss, his gain.

Roy climbed in and shut the door behind. Turning the key, the engine quickly kicked over and started. Not the sexiest car, Roy thought, but it seemed to run well and was a couple of years newer than his current model.

Roy pulled out and headed for the exit. He wondered several things: Did the guard know the car and who owned it? Did anyone ever leave at this time of day? Would he have to stop and show some sort of pass or badge? As he neared the shack, he noticed the guard reading a magazine. Plus, he faced the entrance and away from the exit lane. He was probably more concerned about the cars arriving than the ones leaving. He looked up briefly over his shoulder as Roy drove past. Roy waved, and he waved back—then back to his magazine.

Roy was out of the parking lot and down the road. That was too easy, he thought.

Roy drove home and pulled the car around to the back of house—out of sight from the road. Here, he could inspect it better. It was not a bad car for a compact. Nothing special, but a little clean up would do wonders. The plates were still good for another seven months. Roy would need to make sure dirt got splattered in all the right places to hide most of the letters and numbers. Wow—a new car. He'd abandoned his old outside of the factory. It had been stolen, too, so no need to worry about it. The new one was better. Besides, beggars (thieves?) cannot be choosers.

Roy's old man noticed the car as soon as he got home. He was drunk, of course, but not too drunk to see an unfamiliar vehicle parked at his house. He came in as Roy sat on the sofa in front of the TV.

"What the hell? Another little piece of shit car out back?" He slammed the door.

"I picked it up today."

"Stole it, didn't you?"

"No."

"Don't lie to me. You ain't got no money."

"I did some favors for a guy."

"Favors? What'd you do—some homo shit?"

"No!"

"I think you did some homo shit. Get rid of the fucking car."

"It's mine!"

"No stolen cars here. I ain't going to jail."

"It's not stolen."

His dad picked him up by his shirt. "Get your ass out there and get that fucking car out of here." He punched Roy in the eye. Roy went down. His dad kicked him in the ribs. It hurt. "Piece of shit! Stealing cars." He kicked again. It hurt worse. Then he picked Roy up and threw him out the door. Roy landed on the grass and rolled. "Get the fuck out of here!"

Roy jumped in the car and got out of there. Down the road, he pulled over. He tried really hard not to cry, but he couldn't help it. The pain—and shame—was too great.

Roy kept the car. He figured, what the hell. What was the old man going to do? Beat him up? That happened anyway, and he'd been beat up for much less: not cleaning the dishes good enough; not bringing in the garbage cans; not unclogging the toilet; to name a few. It took very little. At least this way he'd have a decent car. Roy began the process of painting it and changing it up some.

Within a month, he had it repainted. It wasn't a great job, not even a good one, but it changed the appearance enough. And with a new spoiler on the trunk, and a racing stripe down the entire length of the car from bumper to bumper, it looked as gaudy as hell, but if it saved getting pulled over, so be it.

His old man actually said nothing more about the car. Roy couldn't figure it out, but maybe because it kept him busy and out of the old man's hair. That and being productive. Whatever the case, Roy never brought it up, and neither did he.

Roy was wise enough to head in the opposite direction on his next school "vacation" day. He took the train—something told him to leave his car at home. Besides, the train was cheap enough and he could catch a ride west in the morning and pick up an eastbound train towards evening. Easy. Besides needing some down time away from school, Roy was "shopping" for a new stereo system for his car. The one currently installed was stock, and he wanted something with a little more bite to it.

He got off the train at the Mansfield Depot and walked up the hill to downtown—town square was more like it. Roy had his backpack with him to carry his needed tools and to carry his new stereo back home. It was turning into a sunny and warm day, and Roy spent an hour lollygagging around the square. There were no prospective donors for his project, so by noon he was out of town about a mile toward the suburbs. There he found a shopping complex complete with a large chain department store and a Big Market. Plenty of cars graced the parking lot. He'd slowly walk down a row, keeping his eyes peeled for potential prospects, and then he'd go inside or sit on a bench outside before doing another swoop down the next aisle of cars.

During the third row passed, he found a really nice Power Blaster, but the owner had parked up front—second car from the end—and it was a little too risky, even for Roy. Damn the luck, he thought, taking his seat on the bench. About that time, a 4 x 4 truck—pretty red—came rocking down the strip. It was blasting a loud classic rock tune—and it sounded pretty good, even from the outside. The bass was booming, and Roy figured the driver—a thirty-something male—was pretty much begging Roy to take the music machine off of his hands.

Roy watched him park far away from all the other cars (not wanting a door ding, most likely) in the last row, and he even backed in so the rear wheels went off the asphalt and into the hill of grass. The truck tilted frontward and the show-off driver jumped out. He had a work uniform on and headed toward the store, presumably for his work shift. Perfect, Roy thought. Roy lit a cigarette to give the guy some time, just in case he was only running in for his paycheck or something. Roy was no dummy. He could wait another ten minutes or so.

After putting out the last of his cigarette, Roy walked lazily toward the red truck. Behind it were some woods that led back toward the town square, and the highway was next to it. The last spot on the last row in the corner. Roy went to the far side of the truck and looked inside. The stereo was a beautiful aftermarket model, mounted below the dash, held on by a nut and bolt on either side. Easy pickings. Roy moved off toward the woods a few steps to get his adjustable wrench and wire cutters out of his backpack. There were various rocks scattered about, and Roy selected one about the size of a softball.

He went back to the truck, knowing he'd have to move quickly. When he smashed the rock into the driver's window, it shattered and set off the auto alarm. It sounded like an air raid warning and was loud. Roy quickly open the door. He dove under the dash and onto the floorboard. The wrench found the first nut, and he loosened it. While turning the nut off with his fingers, he loosened the second nut with the wrench. Roy had them both off in a matter of seconds, and the unit fell to the floor. With wire cutters, he snipped the speaker wires, the power supply, and the antenna lead. The stereo was loose. Roy picked up the two nuts, squirmed back out of the truck, and wiped the inside of the door latch with his shirtsleeve. Then he quickly wiped off the exterior handle. He had touched nothing else, so no prints. He only wished the stupid alarm would shut the hell up. It was as loud as hell.

As Roy stashed the stereo and his tools into his backpack, he saw the driver and a security guard running out of the store. The driver was yelling, and the guard was on his walkie-talkie—both hurrying towards him. Roy slipped on the backpack and tore into the woods. It was thick coverage—which was good—but not the easiest to negotiate. The sound of the alarm faded and the sound of a squad car grew. Roy saw the police car roar past and most likely heading toward the truck.

FIVE

Roy blasted out of the trees and found himself in the town square. He crossed over and moved down the hill toward the train depot. Not too far to go now — as long as no one had seen him. A train was boarding as he approached the station and he heard the "All aboard!" call. The police siren was now growing in volume, and he was sure they were coming his way.

Roy slowed as he entered the depot — not wanting to look too suspicious. He calmly walked through to the other side and gave the train attendant his return pass as he jumped aboard. Roy grabbed a window seat and sat low. The police car went screaming past, but it didn't stop.

Hurry, Roy thought. Get this fucking train moving.

The squad car turned around down the block and came back toward him. Just then, he felt the train moving. They were pulling away from the station as the squad car stopped and two officers jumped out. They looked around the station. One officer began talking to a gentleman sitting at a bench, but by now the train was moving down the tracks. Roy watched as the police and their car got smaller and smaller — the train picking up speed. It turned a bend and Roy could see the station no more. He smiled and sat back in his seat.

• • •

Two weeks later, Patty found herself at Roy's house. Well, his dad's house, actually.

"Your dad's not home?" she asked.

"Hardly ever. Which is just how I like it." He sat on the sofa and Patty sat next to him. The TV came to life: some game show. "Yeah, he is usually only here to sleep. Otherwise, it's work or the bar—that's about it for the old son-of-a-bitch." Roy put his arm around her. It wasn't the first time, but it was the most solitary place they had been where he put his arm around her. Over the course of the last two weeks, and being together almost every night, they'd made out (just kissing) in his car a couple of times. Aunt Meredith was not too happy about all the time they were spending together, but Patty found out Roy didn't have any friends, and since neither did she, well, there you are.

"He sounds kind of like my dad, too, but I'm never staying with him anymore," she said.

"If I'm here when the old man gets home, he'll smack me around a bit." He paused. "Quite a bit, actually. So I either leave or wait until I know he has already made it home and passed out. My mom's gone, but she wasn't much better. She never slept—nag nag nag nag." He looked at me. "You know what I mean?"

"I used to call my mom The Witch," she said. "Of course, I call my dad The Monster, but that's another story." (Dr. Alice would so proud. Patty had found someone, and they had a lot in common.)

Roy leaned in and kissed her, which was fine, but he seemed in a hurry—not relaxed, and he seemed to have extra energy, almost like he was nervous. After only two quick kisses, his hand moved to the front of her shirt—unbuttoned and inside in a second.

Colors exploded in Patty's head. Red flash—white flash—the fog moved in quickly, but the colors continued. She was immediately outside herself. She was away from her body. Detached. More explosions. Blue flash—yellow flash. In focus, then out-of-focus. Back again. Everything became small and far away. Faster and faster—closing in all around—closing in on her. Faster and faster. Closer and closer. No room. Cannot breathe. Choking. Choking. She thrashed her arms about. She needed air. Kicking out with her legs. She needed space. Screaming screaming screaming.

"Whoa whoa whoa! Calm down, Patty."

It was Roy. He was standing over her. She was on the floor. She didn't remember getting there. A trail of blood snaked down from his nose and he held his hand to it. The blood spilling down his fingers, his wrist. He grabbed an old T-shirt, crumpled on a chair and held it to his nose.

"Jesus, Patty. What's wrong with you?" he asked. "A simple 'no' works, you know."

She was breathing heavy. On her butt, sitting up, but on the floor. Her heart was pumping fast. No memory of getting there. Lost. Confused.

"You OK?" he asked.

She nodded slowly. "What happened?"

"All I did was put my hand on your tit and you went ballistic. Look what you did to my fucking nose."

"Oh, I'm sorry." Then she got mad. "No, I'm not! Keep away from my breasts. I'd like you to take me home now."

"OK, sorry." He checked the T-shirt. "Can I at least wait until my nose stops bleeding?"

"I need to go now." And she headed for the door.

That time at Roy's dad's house was the first time that whole blacking out thing happened. It wasn't the last.

"You're the first girl to draw blood," Roy had said later. "Pretty impressive."

She wasn't mad at Roy—well, yes; she was—but she was mostly mad that it happened. And why it happened.

She still saw him after that—she couldn't help it since he was her lab partner and all. (And her with no other friends, remember?) He actually cleaned his new car out for her—no more burger bags and cigarette wrappers, smashed beer cans and old coffee cups, and on and on. She figured the car was stolen, and she never understood why he wouldn't have stolen something nicer. And the paint job was a little much.

"Next time I get a car, I'll get you something really nice," he said.

Patty thought maybe he cleaned his car so they had more room to move about—especially the back seat—and because they spent so much time back there and moving about. Besides doing a little homework when she got the urge, she spent most of her time in his car—making out. But that was as far as it went. Every time he tried to go further, she'd freak out on him. Get that blacked-out rage thing going. She supposed it challenged him and it intrigued him. But she'd blank out and start swinging and kicking whenever he tried anything. Patty couldn't help it.

It was the last day of school and time for a celebration. Roy got a twelve pack and for Patty he bought (stole?) a bottle of peppermint schnapps.

"This stuff is pretty good," she said. She'd never had any before—not too much of a drinker, actually—but she felt like celebrating since she passed and was now a sophomore. Roy would be a senior. He had actually passed—squeaking by with solid D's. He seemed to have a knack for knowing just how far he could push something before backing off and getting away with it.

They sat in his car at Lumbar Park. Soft music playing on the radio. Seats reclined all the way back, so they were actually in the back seat.

"Norton Construction is hiring workers. I think I might check it out. You think I can pass for eighteen?" he asked.

"Twenty, probably," she said. "That would be great if they hired you." She filled another cup of schnapps—on ice—going down smooth. After two more cups (and a dozen kisses), she was feeling lightheaded, and somewhat giddy.

"I need another drink," she slurred a little, and then she giggled. And then she hiccupped. Which meant another giggle.

"Feeling pretty good there, Patty?"

She took another sip and leaned her head back, exposing her neck. "I is feeling fine."

Roy leaned in and kissed her neck. Patty giggled again, and her hand reached down to his jeans. He jumped slightly, which she liked. Her hand moved around some, and his hand moved to her jeans. Nothing triggered for her. Amazing.

"I'm still here," she said. "Don't stop."

He didn't. Tangled arms and legs. Jeans coming down. She pulled his shirt off. He had nice muscles. He pulled her shirt off, stopped for a second, and looked down at her.

"Yes," she said. "Still here. Love me, Roy."

She felt warm. Relaxed. She opened up. It wasn't like the other times before. This was nicer. Softer. Roy tried to make it last, but it was over as quick as it started. He was breathing heavily and rolled off of her. "God, Patty. That was incredible."

"It was very nice," she said. Her head started spinning. The car started spinning. She opened her door and vomited outside on the ground. A jogger across the field noticed her and her nakedness. He stopped and gawked. Patty didn't even care. She flipped him off, wiped her lower lip, and closed the door again. Her cheek found Roy's chest — warm muscles — a masculine scent — nice — and she fell asleep.

After she was allowed to have it happen one time — sex, that is — the second time went just fine — fine indeed. No trancing out — and she wasn't stone-cold drunk either. Patty guessed she was glad about it — but not near as glad as Roy. He wanted to try again and again.

"They're scientific experiments. To make sure everything is still working," he said.

"Seems to be working just fine," she replied.

And off they'd go again. Patty didn't know if it would work with someone else or not.

"And we don't fucking need to worry about THAT either," Roy said.

SIX

"What kind of experience do you have?"

Roy shrugged. "I always fix the stuff my old man breaks at the house—which is everything at one time or another." He paused. "He breaks everything he touches."

The man just sat and stared.

"I've built decks," Roy continued. "And worked on roofs. I'm real good with my hands. I'm not afraid to get dirty, and I'm super reliable. Give me a shot. Hell, if I don't work out, just fire me."

"Yeah, well, I can do that." The man, Mr. Bergman, sat back in his chair. "Todd says he knows you, and he says, well, something like 'Be careful.' What's he mean by that?"

"I don't know. I never hung with Todd—only knew him from school. I wouldn't think he knows that much about me. I had a shop class with him. He made a really nice wooden table, I remember. I made a low table for our living room. He seemed to like it at the time."

"Yeah, he mentioned that table of yours. Said it was impressive." Mr. Bergman sat and thought for a moment. "All right. I'll give you a chance. But be on time—on time is being early—and show up every day—otherwise, like you said—it's the highway. Start tomorrow at seven—six fifty."

"Yes, sir." Roy smiled. "You won't be disappointed."

Mr. Bergman nodded. "Let's hope not."

· · ·

Roy's newly painted old compact pulled up in front of Aunt Meredith's place.

"Aunt Meredith! I'm going out," Patty yelled as she ran out the front door toward his car. She jumped in and they drove off.

"Aunt Meredith is happy you got the construction job."

Roy smirked. "She's just glad you won't be hanging around with me during the day—only in the evenings." He was sweaty, and dirty, and tired, and drinking a beer.

Patty shook her head. "That's not true. She likes you well enough." She watched Roy slurp some beer. Seemed like he drank beer every night now.

"Construction makes you really thirsty," Roy claimed. "Shit, the first beer does nothing but knock the dust down your throat. The second one you can actually taste." They got to his dad's house and took their places on the sofa. Game show on the TV at low volume. Roy on Beer Number 3. (Could be 4 or 5 for all Patty knew.) A loud truck pulled up outside. "Holy shit. My old man's home."

Patty had never met Roy's father, and she didn't know if she wanted to now. "What do we do?"

"Nothing to do now except hang on. You never know who'll walk through the door. It's early, so maybe we'll be in luck."

He walked in through the kitchen. Slammed the back door. Stood in the corner. "Why the hell didn't you take the trash cans out this morning!"

"Dad, it's not Monday."

Two steps to Roy and then a backhand across the mouth. "If I want any lip from you, I'll damn-well will ask for it."

Roy had taken the blow, but he quickly righted himself. "Get out, dad. Not in front of my girl."

He looked at Patty. "Who the hell are you?"

"Hello, sir. My name is Patty."

He snarled. "Yeah? What the hell do you see in this piece of shit?"

Then he backhanded Roy again. Roy jumped back up and grabbed Patty's hand. He said nothing, but led her out the front door. She saw his nose trickling blood again. His father was yelling Get The Fuck Back Here, but they kept moving, and the old man didn't follow.

Down the road a couple of blocks, Roy pulled over. He was furious—huffing and puffing, nose dribbling, eyes even watering. "I hate that son-of-a-bitch. I hate him."

Patty sat quietly.

"That's the last time," Roy said.

. . .

The next day, Roy was later than normal when he picked her up.

"I got a surprise for you," he said.

They drove to the old part of town — over by the train tracks — and he parked the car behind an old 3-story building. He ran around to her side of the car and opened the door for her. Weird.

He grabbed her hand, and they entered the building from the back. Up the stairs they went. The stairs were old and wooden, and creaked at almost every step. At the second floor landing were a couple of doors and a couple of trash cans by each. Stinky, too. They continued to the third floor and Roy pulled out a key. He opened one of the two doors and spread out his hand.

"Welcome to my castle," he said. She looked at him and then looked inside. "I got my own place. Check it out." He pulled her in. It wasn't much, but Roy sure was excited.

"This is the living room." Two folding chairs, wood floor, window with an old pull-down shade — brownish — probably used to be white.

"Here is the kitchen." Just off the living room, space for a table — that wasn't there — and a refrigerator — old style — the refrigerator was. He opened the refrigerator door. Bare except for a twelve pack. "Would you like a beverage?" he asked. She shook her head. He grabbed a can and popped the top. Slurped some down.

"And back here is the bedroom." More wood flooring and another window with a brown/white shade. A small bed — and actually neatly made with a red football team blanket on top — complete with two pillows.

"I need you to decorate for me," Roy said. "What do you think? I told you no more old man. I got my own place. Cool, huh?"

She smiled. "Yeah, it's pretty nice. Good for you."

A train rumbled by and shook the entire building. The deafening roar made it impossible to talk. Roy was laughing, but she couldn't hear him. Finally, the train passed.

"The place has its quirks," he said.

He knocked her over onto the bed. Got on top of her. "Wanna try it out?"

So they did.

The eagle soars high
Not a care in the sky
Looking for its prey

The butterfly is low
Unsure of its path
Looking for its way

Across the street from Roy's new (?) apartment, and situated right next to the railroad tracks, was Matt Lou's Tattoos. One evening, Roy dragged Patty over to Lou's. He said he wanted a tattoo, and she should get one, too.

"No way," she said.

"You'll see. It won't be bad."

The potential artwork was on display across the wall behind the counter. Matt Lou occupied a stool in front. It was fairly dark in the place. Hard rock music from the '70s played—and not in the background—it was pretty much front and center. Lou turned it down a notch when they entered. He had a tank top on and jeans, and every inch of his visible skin was full of ink of some type or another. This included his neck, but the ink stopped at his hairline, his earlobes, and his jaw.

"My man," Matt Lou said. "What can I do you for?"

"We both want a tattoo."

"No, I don't," Patty said.

"You can get a little one, Patty—out of the way. It will be cool. Like we are joined together by ink." He pointed at the displays. "I was thinking of getting that eagle. And see that little blue butterfly? That would look great right here." He touched her jeans below the belt. She swatted his hand away.

"Not interested," she said.

· · ·

It hurt like hell. They both said it wouldn't—the little liars. Roy went first and got his eagle, and he didn't squirm or scream or anything, so Patty thought it must not be too bad. Now she realized he was faking it the whole time. It hurt like hell. His eagle was below his underwear line and was about four inches from bald head to tip of tail feather, and from wing tip to wing tip. It was on his front, but toward his left side.

"Now, Patty, your turn. Your little butterfly can be on the right side. That way, the eagle can kiss the butterfly. Pretty cool, huh?"

That was his idea of romance.

It was her idea of pain. Pain that continued for a while afterwards, too. And the tattoo was more red than blue, at least until the swelling went down. Damn him.

After a couple of weeks, though, whenever she'd peek at it below her bikini line, she had to admit she kind of liked it. *The Eagle and the Butterfly,* she thought. *That was us.*

One flies high
Softly Silently Smoothly
One flies low
Flitters Jitters but still silent
The two so different
The two so together

What a difference a year makes. Last year Patty was a new freshman at a new school. She knew no one. This year, a sophomore with a boyfriend who has his own car and own place. (Although she still didn't have any other friends to speak of. She had kind of talked to Rachel a few times, and they were friendly toward each other, but they never really hung out or saw each other outside of school. Patty had tried to talk to Bob a few times, but he always seemed a bit leery.) Roy didn't want to come back to school. He figured construction work was as good a job he'd have for a while, so no point in going to school, right? She didn't know if she agreed with him or not, but it seemed to be the right move for him. Patty considered not going back herself, since she was spending more and more time at his place now. He was basically supporting her. But Aunt Meredith would have no part of Patty not going to school.

"You WILL stay in school, young lady," she said. "And get good grades, and get your driver's license, and do all the normal things a teenage girl should do. How about going to a dance? Doesn't that sound like fun?" She paused as she shook her head. "You are growing up way too fast."

• • •

In hindsight, William Lancaster knew his anger and frustration went back at least a couple of years. His work had become increasingly stressful. William worked in sales for a medical supply company, and sales were down and so was he. He started working for Anderson Medical Supply right out of college—that had been ten years now (seemed like twenty). He worked his way up from Cubicle 12 all the way to Cubicle 1—faster than anybody in the history of Anderson, in fact. And it was all because of hard work and long hours—especially the long hours. William had no outside life. He had no outside hobbies. It was by a fluke that he had even met Maggie.

William rarely went to any kind of social function. It all seemed pointless to him. He was with plenty of people while at work. Being alone was always more relaxing after hours.

But that one day Earl Nolan had insisted. Earl was the closest thing William had to a friend, but that was only because, as a co-worker, they spent a substantial amount of time together. Outside of work, Earl had a family and a life. And the upcoming weekend, Earl was having a barbeque.

"Look, William. I'll be totally offended if you don't show up on Saturday. I'm not asking you to stay for long. Drink a beer. Have a brat. And you can be on your way. OK?"

And so on his way to Earl's, that was William's plan, too: one beer, one brat, one way back home.

On Saturday, he found a lawn chair and sat down. Several vacant lawn chairs surrounded him. He was glad they were vacant. Across the grass—a good twenty feet away—was another contingent of lawn chairs, these with people occupying them. There were maybe twenty people. Two people from work: Mary and Natalie. And with them, they had husbands (or dates). And then, of course, Earl Nolan. He spotted William right away and immediately went straight to him.

"You made it, William!" He was grinning. "I'll be damn. Honestly—I didn't think you'd show."

William said nothing.

"Let me get you a beer. The brats aren't done yet." Earl hustled over to the coolers. He grabbed a beer out of the big blue cooler. It was dripping with ice and water. Then grabbed a girl by her elbow and brought her and the beer back to William. Popping the can, he said, "William, I'd like you to meet my cousin—Maggie."

"Hi, William," she said, and when she grinned, a dimple appeared on her left cheek.

"Hi." William took the beer from Earl. Maggie took a vacant lawn chair next to William. And Earl took off—the ass.

"Earl has told me a lot about you," Maggie said. "He said you're like the hardest worker."

· · ·

Maggie talked a lot. Period. And when she got nervous or scared or excited, she talked even more. The day she met William at Earl's barbeque, excitement was in the air for her. She rarely met any available guys, so whenever she did, her nerves got the best of her.

"So, are you like the hardest worker at Anderson?" she said to William. Earl had slinked away and left the two of them alone. William's eyes had followed Earl as he walked off, then he focused on Maggie.

"Oh, I don't know if I'd say that," he said. "I do my part."

"He told me you are always there. No one can get there earlier than you in the morning, and no one stays later at night. I like that. A good strong work ethic. It says a lot about a man, you know. Responsibility. Integrity. Accountability. And cute, too." She giggled. William blushed.

"What is it you do?" he asked.

"I work at the elementary school—Parkville Elementary. I'm the one who answers the phone when people call. You'll find me at the front desk in the office, so I'm the first person people talk in person, too. I get to talk to a lot of people. It's fun and never really gets boring.

And you know what else? I'm the person who opens the door when someone comes to the entrance and pushes the button. 'Hello, may I help you?' I say, and then they tell me their business. Then I decide if they have a right to come in or not. I can see them on the camera. And then I push a button and the door swings open and they come in — to talk to me in person. I've never NOT let someone in, but one of these days, you never know, I might save the school and have to put it on lock-down. Kind of like a secret agent, right?"

William nodded. And smiled. Maggie was in paradise. They talked the rest of the night, and when evening closed, William had somehow found the courage to ask Maggie out on a date. She agreed immediately.

SEVEN

And then there was that first night Patty didn't come home from his apartment. It was snowing pretty badly, and the roads were getting slicker and slicker. She called Aunt Meredith. "I'm just going to stay here tonight, Aunt Meredith. I can walk to school from here if I need to—that is, if there is even school tomorrow."

"No—I'll come get you."

Patty knew she didn't really want to get out in this mess. She pleaded with Aunt Meredith and told her she was OK—not to worry—please don't get out in this mess. You'll get stuck or worse, go in a ditch, or wreck your car. I'm fine here, and I'm closer to school if I need to get there tomorrow.

She finally said, "OK. Just be a good girl."

That seemed almost too easy. It ended up snowing quite a bit—no school—and three nights at Roy's. After that, staying over at Roy's became more and more customary (as long as she was a good girl). Patty held her grades at C's and B's—no A's—but no D's or F's either—passable.

As the weeks dragged on, she decorated Roy's place somewhat. He came across a nice flat screen TV and two easy chairs. (They didn't match—but both were comfortable.) The kitchen stayed table-less. They always ate in front of the flat screen, so no big deal there. The refrigerator became the biggest problem. Not that it didn't work, but that it was always full of beer, and not much else. Roy was drinking every night and getting drunk, too. She didn't like it. Too much like the Monster.

"Roy, how about stopping with the beer for the rest of the night?"

It was another snowy February night. He had been off work because of the weather, so the beer drinking had begun earlier in the day. He was smashed by the time he picked her up from school. (They had no more snow days.)

"Can't stop," he said. "If I stop, I'll fall right to sleep. And we got things to do, you know." He kissed her hard and grabbed her ass with both hands, pulling her close. It was not romantic nor appreciated. For the first time (since the last bloody nose) Patty pushed him away. "No, Roy. Not when you are so drunk."

She had seen the rage flare up before, but always at someone else. This time, he directed it at her.

"Don't you tell me NO, you little bitch!" Next came the first time he hit her. It was a backhand (like father, like son) across her right cheek. She didn't know if it was the force or the surprise that knocked her over—but she went down. Immediately he was upon her—straddling her with his knees on her biceps—his crotch in her face—and a sneer on his lips. "I get you food, a place to sleep, and nice stuff all the time. And you tell me NO!"

She couldn't move—at least her upper half. Her bottom half was free, and she kicked and flailed her legs, and bucked like a wild horse. This only amused Roy, and he started laughing and yelling, "Ride 'em, cowboy! Yee hah!"

More bucking and rocking. Patty was trancing out like before, but she was stuck because there was no stopping him or getting him off of her. Patty could not handle being unable to move. It freaked her out. Flashes and bright colors. Spinning and spinning. The world closing in. Getting smaller and smaller and smaller. And then the blackness.

She woke up later—don't know how long it had been. She was on the living room floor. Her shirt was on (but ripped and open), and her jeans and panties crumpled on the floor across the room. Bastard. He was asleep in the bed—sideways—and naked—snoring. She stared at him—considering if she should kill him. Kitchen knife in the chest. At the thought, her hands shook furiously. She knew she could never do it.

She took a shower. Washed it all away. And slept in one of the living room chairs.

.　　.　　.　　.

Patty awakened in the early morning.

"I'm so sorry, Patty. God, I'm so sorry." Roy was crying. He was on his knees in front of the chair. "Please forgive me. I didn't know what I was doing. I won't do it again. I love you so much." He buried his face with tears in her lap.

She reached down and slowly stroked his hair. But she knew she needed to be back at Aunt Meredith's.

Dating was such a nerve-wracking thing for William. He'd always find himself trying to get the courage to ask the next thing, do the right thing, go to the next level; knowing all along it could backfire on you and you'd never see the girl again. Not that William had that much experience. In fact, Maggie was the first "real" serious date he ever had. The couple of gang dances he did in high school — where three or four guys went with three or four girls — all too chicken to step out and make any kind of commitment to someone else — these didn't count.

The first date with Maggie went well enough. They had made their way to a bar and grill, famous for a variety of special hamburgers, all served with ragin' Cajun fries, with an opening round of their equally famous house salad. Maggie dressed in slightly tight jeans, and a blue button up blouse that was slightly tight, too. Gold circles for earrings, and a matching necklace with a gold circle pendent that hung at the start of her cleavage. She caught William staring at her cleavage, and when he looked up, he quickly said, "Nice necklace."

"Nice recovery," she said.

And when he replied with, "What?"

She just said, "Never mind."

William quickly changed the subject, but in hindsight, he realized he probably shouldn't have told her she had a bit of lettuce stuck to her front tooth. It was so hard not to stare at it. Maggie talked a lot and whenever her lip snuck up past her front tooth—there it was.

She noticed him not looking at her eyes, but down a bit—and not as far as her necklace. "Something wrong, William?"

"No, no, no." He shook his head. He looked back at her and she grinned. And there was the lettuce again. "It's just that you have some lettuce, or something green, on your front tooth there."

"Oh, my." She whipped her head around to face the other way, and he saw her bring her napkin to her mouth. When she looked back, she was silent. And she never touched her salad again.

William said something along the lines that he would have wanted to know, and then graciously—smartly—changed the subject. When she finally spoke again, he noticed—nonchalantly—that the lettuce had disappeared.

He had had fun—she was definitely easy to talk to—and wanted to go out again. But to ask her meant opening himself up for rejection. Did she like him enough to go out again?

"Um," he said at the front door of her apartment. It was a three story complex, and she was in Apartment K on the third level. "Um, I had fun tonight."

Maggie paused for a second. William began to sweat. Finally— "Me, too."

Hmm—a good sign.

"Would you like to go out again?" he asked. "Can I call you? Is next weekend OK?"

Maggie giggled. He saw the little dimple (and no lettuce!) on her cheek.

"Three questions at once."

"Sorry. My mind is going really fast."

"Yes, let's go out again. Yes, please call me. Yes, next weekend is open." A smile. A dimple.

He exhaled. No rejection! "Great. I'll call you." Now the mystery of the kiss. Should he or shouldn't he?

"OK. I look forward to your call."

Screw it. He was going for it. He leaned in and gave her the quickest, lightest kiss in the history of the modern world. William might have grazed her lips, but was sure the kiss was mostly side of mouth/cheek.

"Was that OK?" he asked. "Do you still want to go out?"

Another giggle. Another dimple. Then her left hand reached out and held the back of his neck. She leaned up and planted a full kiss on his lips. William bet it was every bit of twenty seconds. Then she leaned back, released his neck, turned, and disappeared behind the door.

William thought that must have meant "yes." He turned and floated down the flights of steps to his car.

•   •

The doorbell rang at Aunt Meredith's house. She and Patty were finishing their dinner.

"Now who could that be?" Aunt Meredith went to the door and then returned with Roy. He had a sheepish grin on his face, and a present tucked under his arm.

"Hi, Patty," he said. "Can I talk to you for a minute?"

She wiped her mouth with a napkin, and the two of them moved to the living room.

"I got you a little something," he said. "I feel really bad about what happened the other night. I know you are really mad, and I don't blame you one bit, but I wanted to give you something to remind you I still care about you and will wait until the end of time for you."

Please, Roy. Talking sappy song lyrics does not become you. Patty took the present he extended and opened it. Inside was a necklace with an eagle on the end, holding onto a good-sized diamond within its talons.

"That's the eagle, you know, meaning to be me."

"I get it, Roy. Thank you."

"Let's try it on, OK?"

He took it from the box and placed it around her neck. Then he kissed her on the cheek. "I'm sorry, honey," he whispered.

Patty nodded and watched him get up in silence and walk to the door. Before he walked out, he turned, smiled, and mouthed another "I'm sorry."

She nodded again, and he left.

•   •

"Well, I have to admit—can I say it?—I'm glad you're on the outs with Roy." Aunt Meredith stood over her with her arms crossed. Patty sat quietly at the table. "I guess I shouldn't say that." She rested her hand on Patty's shoulder. "I just love you and worry about you, and you're spending way too much time with that boy—man—I should say." She sat down across from her. "He doesn't have the greatest reputation, you know."

"Look," she said. "He's a nice guy. Leave him alone and leave me alone, too. OK?"

Aunt Meredith frowned and moved some dishes to the kitchen sink. "I'll shut up about it," she said. "I just want to do right by your mother—God rest her soul—and sometimes I think I am failing."

· · ·

On reflection, moving in with Aunt Meredith had been her only option—other than getting involved in social services. No thanks. She was her mom's only sister—younger—no brothers, and Monster Dad had no siblings. None that Patty knew about anyway, or would want to live with, that's for sure. Aunt Meredith was nice enough. Patty used to visit her when she was younger, when she was still married to Uncle Kevin. He was nice, too—probably her favorite. Always told funny jokes—really corny dad jokes actually, but sometimes those are the best ones. The best thing was he'd always treated her like an adult and not some kid.

The first couple of months she lived with Aunt Meredith, the two of them hung around quite a bit. Aunt Meredith worked for a chiropractor's office—Dr. Franklin—checking people in, hooking up the e-stem machine, and making appointments. Forty hours a week spread out over six days. When she was off, they cooked meals together, went into town to the mall, and usually saw a movie every other weekend. After school started, Aunt Meredith met Nathan, and he then took up most of her spare time. She tried to include Patty a couple of times, but that was just weird. A third wheel. Patty ended up being home alone a lot more after that, and, of course, Roy had soon entered the picture—so that became her life.

· · ·

Maggie could not resist giggling when William proposed to her. Not that she thought it funny, but rather, an indication of the joy she actually felt. Her joy always manifested itself in a giggle (and a dimple, of course).

"Yes, I'll marry you, William. How sweet of you to ask." She giggled and helped William up. He had been kneeling on his right knee. When he slid the smallish ring on third finger left hand, she giggled again. "This is so exciting. I'll have to call my mom and my sister. They'll be excited, too. What kind of wedding do you want? It'll have to be fairly small—we don't have many friends, you know." A short giggle this time. "All the people from your work—cousin Earl, of course, the little matchmaker—and all my people from school. When do you want to do this? Soon?"

Soon it was. Three months from the day, in fact. A smallish wedding at a Lutheran church. ("Lutherans have the prettiest weddings, don't you think, William?") The reception was at the local VFW Hall. A country/reggae band, The Rastafari Bumpkins, provided the music. It wasn't country/reggae music, but one country song followed by one reggae song, mixing in a slow one of each genre periodically. It actually worked pretty well. The singer had a long eight-inch beard, matched with long dreadlocks. A perfect country reggae mix. The guitarist looked like the middle-aged guy next door, and the drummer could have passed for his son, and probably was. His kit consisted of only a bass drum, snare, and a high hat. Slim pickings, but he played them well, and the songs did not lack for any other drums. The bass player was on a double bass, and he spun it around occasionally to great effect.

The new Lancaster couple received many wonderful gifts, some before the wedding at a shower, some at the wedding itself, and a few post ceremony/reception—mostly for their new home—but one of their favorites was the way several people had kicked in to buy a honeymoon trip for them: three days in the Bahamas.

They spent their wedding night at a fairly swanky hotel in a suite. Maggie had drunk way too much champagne, and the room was spinning, especially after she started jumping on the bed and twirling around like a ballerina—laughing the whole time until she crashed down onto the soft mattress. She laughed some more and raised her legs—kicking them back and forth. Her beautiful, white wedding dress fell down to her waist, and her exposed ankles, calves, and thighs were too much for William. Instantly, his tux became a ball of fabric in the corner and he stood naked in front of her. Well, not quite. In his rush, he had forgotten the black bow tie; so there he stood at attention—looking every bit like some silly male dancer.

Maggie stopped kicking long enough to look at William. It was the first time she had seen William naked. (Well, except for the one accidental intrusion on his shower a month prior...) She laughed, giggled one more time, and said, "Come here, big boy."

He was done in an instant; and it was just as well for Maggie, since the room was really spinning now. ("Earth shaking," she later described it to her sister.)

The front desk called two hours later with their wake up call. Their Bahama flight left at 8 a.m., so together they achingly moved in auto drive—both with headaches, red eyes, and, in fact, still drunk. Maggie kept her eye on that little bag in the seat back in front of her during the entire flight, knowing that, perhaps, there may be a first time need to use it. But thankfully, no "ralph-ing" or "bruce-ing" into the bag in route.

The Bahamian airport, tiny and open-aired, reminded them of a parent drop-off station at a high school, but they didn't care. They were in the Bahamas. All they needed now was their hotel shuttle.

"There," William said. "That white van with Electric Beach on the side of it. That's us."

"I see it," Maggie said. Being back on land had helped her headache and disposition, but it was short-lived. They clambered into the van while the driver took their bags.

"Hello there. I am Mateo. Your driver. Welcome to Nassau."

"Aloha—oh, I guess we don't say that here," Maggie said. William just rolled his eyes, hoping maybe Mateo had not heard her from the outside back of the van.

But when Mateo jumped in. "Ah—here in the Bahamas we say 'hello' or 'hi.' Are you Hawaiian?"

William broke in. "No—just a little stupid."

"Hey!" Maggie elbowed William. She had the window seat and William was on the aisle. "Your steering wheel sure looks funny on the right side."

"Yes, we drive on the British side of the road, too," Mateo said. "But everything in the Bahamas is relaxed. Sit back and enjoy and have relaxation." And then in one movement he shifted into drive and bolted out onto the little, narrow, winding street, not bothering to look first, or for that matter, being bothered by the honking of the yellow VW Beetle he had just cut off.

Maggie's headache came back, and she buckled her seat belt. "Is this a long drive to the hotel?"

Mateo grinned. He had a wide smile with large white teeth. "Only twenty miles. We should be there in five or ten minutes."

Maggie straightened up. "Wait..."

"Only a little Mateo joke." Still grinning. "Two miles. Re-la-a-a-x," he said slowly, and they barreled down the road—on the British side.

EIGHT

Roy pulled up to work. The sun was just peaking over the horizon and Roy knew he was actually a few minutes early to work for once. They were usually heading out from the work shed to start up, and the sun was higher in the sky. If he knew he had that much time, he would have gotten some damn coffee. The boss liked him to be fifteen minutes early, but fuck him. If he wanted Roy there early, he'd have to pay him.

Roy turned the car's engine off, but kept the radio on—they were playing some alternative 90s rock song, and Roy figured he'd leave it on, since for once the idiot DJs weren't talking and trying to be funny. Those guys thought they were like the greatest comedians in the world, and they were nothing but idiots, and Roy wished they'd just shut the fuck up and rock. So since they were actually rocking (like two songs every hour), he kept it on and listened. Tom Bergman, his boss, stuck his head out of the work trailer. He motioned for Roy to come over to him. *What the hell*, Roy thought, but he turned off the radio and slowly made his way over to the do-it-yourself wooden steps that led to the inside of the trailer.

"Can I talk to you for a minute?" Tom asked him.

"Yeah," Roy said. What else could he say? Roy entered the trailer—a simple trailer with the inside pretty much gutted except for the bathroom in the middle and an office area on the one end. The rest was one big room that housed a plan table for the blueprints, and a conference table for all the meetings that were held in there with the guys who visited in suits. Tom walked back to the office where there was a desk, one nice desk chair, and then several folding metal chairs.

He indicated for Roy to sit in one of the metal chairs, and Roy did. Tom sat in the desk chair and swiveled to face Roy.

"Roy," he said, "I want to get right to it and see what you might know about it." Roy nodded. "Several air compressor tools showed up missing this past weekend: two nail guns and that nice large staple gun. When did you last see them?"

"Yeah, last Friday." Today was Monday. "I had the staple gun up on the roof with me and was stapling down paper. I'm pretty sure Ron and Todd had the two nail guns inside as they were framing up in the back room."

"Yeah, that's what they said, too." Tom paused. "They said you came and got them and put everything away. They didn't help with that at all, so they said you were the last one to see all three tools."

Roy's upper lip trembled as he started to get angry. "Yeah, that's true," he said. "I put them away, locked up the toolshed and went home." He squinted. "You trying to tell me you think I took 'em?"

Tom raised his palms and shook his head. "No, no. I'm not saying that. I'm just trying to find out who had them last. Are you sure you locked the toolshed?"

"Yeah, I locked it," he said, getting more angry. "It was locked this morning, wasn't it?"

"Well, yeah, and that's just the thing. It *was* locked. If it had been broken into, the door would have been busted, but it was all locked up like the tools were gone before it was locked, or someone forgot to put them away."

"I did not forget to put them away!"

"Well, I can't prove anything." He paused. A long time. "But all I want to say is I'll be watching you." He waited, but Roy said nothing. "If you want to tell me to go to hell and walk away, that's up to you. Otherwise, get out there and go to work."

"Look, Tom," Roy said. "I really need this job. I'm not going to tell you to go to hell. I hope my work speaks for itself."

"You do fine work," Tom said. "So just get out there and do it."

Roy was fuming, but he hid it as best he could. And though he wanted so badly to slam the trailer door when he left, he refrained from doing so, and calmly walked to the tool shed and got his tool pouch.

William couldn't believe Maggie had said *Aloha*. Mateo handled it discreetly, so maybe he had heard it before. Ya mon! No—that's Jamaica.

They survived the van ride to the Electric Beach Hotel. Ocean front room. Twelfth floor. Beautiful day. One enormous bed.

"Let's go to the beach first thing. OK, William?"

He thought of something else he wanted to do first—but pushed himself to patience. It got even harder (?) when Maggie began changing into her swimming suit. Right there in front of him, too.

Maggie strapped on her bikini top. The bottom half still on the bed. She glanced at William, staring. "Are you going to put on your suit, William?" she asked. She cocked her head to one side and put a hand on a hip. "Just nod your head, close your mouth, and get your suit."

William finally turned away. "Ah, sorry. I gotta get used to this married thing." He actually went into the bathroom to change.

Fifteen minutes later, they were on the beach. The beautiful sea in front of them. A cloudless sky overhead. White sand all around. The peaceful lapping of waves every couple of seconds. His wife was lying next to him. They were both oiled up. William could get used to this.

"Can I bring you a drink, sir?" Next to William stood a young man: dark skin, wide smile, large white teeth. William thought he was Mateo for a second. "I am Omario. I work for your hotel."

"Hello, Omario. (No *Aloha*!) I am William. I am relaxing."

"I'm Maggie."

"Hello, pretty lady."

Maggie blushed. "Oh, aren't you sweet?"

"How about something sweet to drink?"

William lifted both his hands. "I did not bring my wallet."

"No problem. Do you know your hotel room number?"

"Twelve twenty-two," Maggie said.

Omario nodded. "I bring you drinks. You sign paper. Go back to relaxing."

"What kind of drinks can I get here? I'm looking for something I can only get here in the Bahamas—and not find anywhere else?"

Omario never stopped smiling. "Yellow bird — very good. Bahama mama — the classic. And for the really brave: a goombay smash."

"What's in a yellow bird?" Maggie asked.

Omario raised and wagged his left index finger. "Ah ah ah ah. No secrets must leave the island. But it is delicious."

William ordered two, and Omario ran off.

"My goodness," Maggie said, looking down the beach in the opposite direction.

William turned to look. A beautiful, well-tanned girl of about twenty was walking toward them. She had a hint of neon green on her lower half, but the wet, white t-shirt on her topside hid no secrets whatsoever from the world. It covered the hint of neon green bottom, but no matching top. Nothing. Just the white wet T-shirt. She was well-endowed and proud of it.

They both watched as she jiggled past them. She was oblivious to the world. She stopped at the chair next to Maggie — ten feet away.

Maggie looked back at William. "Would you please put your eyeballs back in your head — and close your mouth, please?"

"Oh, sorry," he said, and momentarily gazed out to sea. "Not sure why she's wearing that t-shirt. It's useless." He looked back at her for one more peek, and she pulled the t-shirt off and sat down. "Oh, well, that makes sense."

"I forgot some people go topless around here," Maggie said. She unhooked her top, took it off, and placed it next to her. Leaning back, Maggie said, "Close your mouth, William."

He leaned back. "Nice necklace, Maggie."

Just then, Omario was back with their drinks. "Ah, pretty lady. Now you a real Bahama mama. Soaking in the sun the natural way — the Bahamian way. The first drink shall be on the house."

They ended up trying one of each drink, and then they each had one more of their favorite. Maggie's favorite was the yellow bird, and William preferred the goombay smash — although, like Omario said, they were all quite delicious.

They went back to their room feeling pretty tipsy, and feeling pretty loose. They consummated their marriage yet again — a couple of times, actually — and then headed out to dinner.

"I think I better have a soda with dinner," Maggie said after being seated at a table overlooking the beach. The sun was dipping down below the ocean and it was beautiful. A couple of small sailboats were drifting about in the water, and their silhouettes in front of the setting sun made for a picturesque moment. The low tide made for smaller waves, quieter waves, further out to sea, thus creating an extremely large, smooth beach. Sand crabs jittered about. Peaceful. Serene.

"Yeah, but look at this," William said, pointing to the menu. "Soda is six dollars, and the beer is ten. On the way here at the little store, I saw a bottle of rum for seven. Nothing like import tax, I guess. An entire bottle of rum for the same price as a can of soda."

"Oh, dear." Maggie pointed. "A rum and cola is only five—cheaper than the soda. I guess I'll have one of those."

"Me, too."

The drinks came. William eyeballed them suspiciously. "That drink is more clear than dark." He sipped it. "Wow—more rum than cola."

Maggie set her drink down. "Whoa. I can't drink that." She ended up giving hers to William and getting another yellow bird.

Otherwise, the food was delicious. Nothing quite like conch fritters and key lime pie watching a sunset over the ocean in the Bahamas. But William's head was spinning by the time they got back to their room.

"Way too much rum, Maggie. I got to lie down." Which turned into instant sleep.

He awoke in the night. Maggie was snoring next to him. He had a massive headache. And a massive thirst. Middle of the night stumble to the sink. Gotta have water. One glass. Two glasses. Three. Much better. Back to bed and snooze city.

The next morning, Maggie was up first. She tried not to be noisy and wake William, but she failed.

"Hmm. What time is it?"

"It's only eight," Maggie said. "I couldn't sleep. I have a little headache. Go figure, eh?"

"Mine is not little." William slipped out from under the covers and sat on the side of the bed. "I don't feel good at all. Feel like I got a fever."

"I never heard of a hangover with a fever." She came over and felt his forehead. "My — you are burning up."

"Thirsty too. I need more water."

"I'll order some up."

William put his head in his hands. "Oh, shit."

"What's wrong?"

"I drank a bunch of water in the middle of the night — from the sink. I was so thirsty — and pretty drunk."

"William, we aren't supposed to drink the water!"

"Hell, I forgot. I was drunk."

"No wonder you're sick. Lay back down."

He did. More snooze city.

When he awoke, he was still sick. Maggie was pissed.

"What a great honeymoon. My husband, the knucklehead, is sick from drinking the water. What am I supposed to do?"

"No no no." William protested. "I'll get up. We can go to the beach."

He suffered through getting ready and getting to the beach. He found his chair and — no drinks today — fell asleep. If you had to be sick, he guessed no better place than the beach in the Bahamas.

Maggie remained pissed throughout the remainder of the honeymoon, but William started feeling better — slowly — and by the time they were back home — William was at 100% and feeling great. Figures.

• • •

When Roy came back from his lunch break, he sat in his car, radio on. He still had a couple of minutes before twelve thirty and *Back At It*. A black pickup pulled up and coworker Todd Cross jumped out.

"See you after work, Ned," he said to the driver. Roy noticed Ned Schlapinski driving. *I didn't know they hung out*, Roy thought. He had run into Schlapinski just a couple of days ago at the gas station. They had always gotten along decently, and Schlapinski usually had some good smoke.

Roy watched as Cross ran over and entered the work trailer. *What a suck-ass Cross was.*

Roy got out and headed toward the job site where he had left his tool pouch. As he put it on, Tom Bergman came out of the trailer, followed by Cross, who headed off in the other direction toward the lumber pile.

"Hey, Roy!" Bergman yelled. "Can you come over here?"

What now? Roy thought, but slowly made his way over to the trailer. Bergman went inside and Roy followed him in.

They went once again to the back office, and Bergman indicated for Roy to sit in one of the metal chairs. Tom took his desk chair.

"Roy," he said, "I just found out you offered two nail guns and a staple gun for sale to someone. Got anything to say about that?"

That fucking Schlapinski, Roy thought. Roy thought Schlapinski might have been interested in those tools when he saw him at the gas station. He'd offered them to him at a great price. Roy had no idea he was buddies with Cross—who just happened to be Bergman's cousin. *Fuck!*

"Not true."

Bergman stared at his hands, folded them in front of him on the desk. "I thought you might say that."

"Well, it's the truth."

"I see."

"Man, it wasn't me. I'm being framed. Cross has had it out for me since day one. He's making all this shit up."

"Who said anything about Todd?"

Fuck!

"I just saw him leave here. Come on!"

Bergman let out a long, slow breath. "Yep, I can't prove anything." He pulled out a checkbook from his desk. "We're getting kind of slow, Roy. I'm gonna have to let you go."

"This is bullshit!"

"I owe for three days, right?"

"Aw come on, man!"

Bergman wrote out a check.

Roy was fuming—ready to pull someone's head off.

"Here's a check for four days. Get your tools and get outta here."

"You gotta be kidding me! I've been framed!"

"Bye, Roy. And be thankful I don't press charges—which I will if you cause any trouble. Now get your stuff. We're done here."

Roy jumped up and yanked the check from Bergman. He stomped to the door.

"And don't slam the door on you way out!" Bergman called after him.

Roy slammed the door as hard as he could on his way out.

• • •

There was very little William did besides work: work, Maggie, and his yard. He had donated years of his life to this company. And for what? Nothing—that's for sure.

William found himself filling his cup at the coffee machine while talking with coworker Earl Nolan about the natural progression from Cubicle 1 upward to Office 4.

"Man, Office 4 is going to be yours!" Nolan said.

He'd caught William off guard. Office 4—what a sweet deal. It even had a window that looked out over the glorious parking lot—yeah, not much, but at least a window. "What are you talking about?" William asked.

"You didn't hear? It's finally happening. Old Mr. Tosh is retiring at the end of the month." Tosh, of course, was in Office 2, next to Office 1, which belonged to President Anderson, who wasn't ever likely to retire. Office 3 housed Barry Wilson. And Office 4 was the home of Nancy Rather. "So the natural evolution of things: Tosh retires, Wilson moves into Office 2, Rather moves into Office 3 and yes, you, in Cubicle 1, move to Office 4. It's always been that way. That's where Rather came from. You've been here for how many years now? Seven? Hell, you deserve it."

"Ten—feels like twenty—but who's counting?" William said, the light bulb of truth in what Nolan was saying turning on inside his head.

"Congratulations, man. You'll be getting that call into the President's office any day now." Nolan took a big slurp from his coffee. "Right on, man."

That was the beginning of the cloud that seemed to lift William off his feet. He wasn't sure this could really be happening. He figured on being in Cubicle 1 for a long time—well, a longer time, since it had already been a long time. As the logic of Earl Nolan overtook William, he found his steps were lighter, and he couldn't help feeling like he was walking on a cloud. What a good feeling it was, too. Maggie even commented on his good mood when he got home that night.

"What's got into you?" she said. "I haven't seen a smile on your face in months." She had gotten home before him and was preparing something to eat. William had just walked in the door and hadn't realized he was walking around wearing a goofy smile.

"What?" he asked.

"Well, you got a big grin on your face. That is so weird," she said, stirring a steaming crock-pot full of soup with a big spoon.

"Doesn't a man who is getting promoted deserve to smile?"

The big spoon fell to the floor, splattering broth across the floor. Maggie's mouth dropped open. "You got promoted?"

"Well, not yet. But Tosh is retiring and I'm next in line to move to Office 4." William continued to smile and he actually thought that Maggie looked kind of cute with her mouth hanging open as big as the crock-pot. "Cousin Earl told me today, and he said I'm a shoo-in for the promotion. It's always been that way, and always will."

"William, I'm so happy for you. I always told you that your long hours and days and hard work would pay off. You're going to get an office? That is so wonderful. I have to call mom and tell her and call my sister, too. Boy, they'll be surprised. They always thought you were in some dead-end job, but look at you now: an office. Shoot, I wish I wouldn't have made bland old soup. Hey, let's go out and eat. You want to go out and celebrate, William? Let's go get a couple of big old steaks, you want to?" And she was off and running. She didn't stop talking till after they went to the steakhouse, ate, came home, cleaned up and crawled into bed. She was so excited it was as if she herself had gotten the promotion. The last thing she said was "I've never made love to an Office 4 man before." Quite the unusual ending for quite an unusual day—but a good day at that.

· · ·

Maggie was so excited about William's upcoming promotion. Maybe this was exactly what he needed to get out of his funk. Hers, too, for that matter, since she had no kids, zero friends, and not much else to do. At least if William was happier, she'd be happier, and everything would be happier. She could only hope. All she had was William. Well, and her sister.

It was quite a lonely existence, even with all the people she met at the school. These people were all strangers, really. No connection with her except a way to get in to see their kids. Maggie would go home and there was no one. Her sister Martha, yes, but with all her kids and her life, she had little time for Maggie and hers.

Maggie sat alone at the kitchen table, swirling her spoon around in her coffee cup, as she waited for William to get home from work. It wouldn't be long now. Maybe tonight they could have some quality conversation. Maybe tonight they would talk about important things in life. Maybe tonight the television would remain off, and William would remain in the house and not in the yard. Maybe tonight he would tell her all about how great things were at work, how great life was, how great she was, and how excited he was. Maybe tonight. Maybe.

NINE

Yes, Patty was back with Roy. The drinking had stopped since the night he hit her, and things were good again between them. She had a real issue with being around someone drunk. Thanks to The Monster.

Patty found out Roy had lost his job. He said the boss told him business was getting slow, and he was the low man on the totem pole, so he was the first one to get the axe. She could tell it really upset him, but he had taken his last paycheck and cashed it. Then he did what he thought was the best use for the money: he bought a fifth of whiskey. The first drink—on ice—went down fast and smooth. The second one he actually sipped—well, not sipped, but not guzzled either. It seemed the warmth of the drink only served to heat his boiling anger: at Bergman, at Cross—at the whole damn world. By the time he had picked her up from school, he was bottled up and ready to explode.

"That fucking Cross always had it out for me." She and Roy sat in front of the muted TV once again. Patty let him spill it out—knew it would be good for him. She didn't enjoy seeing the bottle slowly drain, but if he ever needed release, she figured this was the time.

"Ever since that time in high school when I accidentally tripped him in the hall. He went down and everybody laughed. I think he wanted to take a swing at me, but then realized he better not. He's been a fuck-turd ever since."

Another refresher to his glass.

"I gotta get even with him somehow."

"Roy, it sounds like they'll press charges if you do anything."

"Fuck that. They don't know who they're messing with."

"Give it some time, please."

"Who the fuck's side are you on?"

"I'm on your side, Roy."

"It doesn't sound like it."

"You're just upset and not thinking clearly, that's all."

Roy jumped. "I'm thinking just fine! You need to back off!"

She raised her hand—in what she thought meant agreement. Roy, on the other hand, took offense.

It was the second time he backhanded her.

Patty went over backward from her chair. She sat up, held her cheek, and looked up at him—she was sure he saw fear—and sadness—in her eyes. "You are scaring me, Roy."

He stepped up to her and slapped the other side of my face. "I said back off!"

"Who is this person? Where is Roy?"

"I'll show you who I am. You want to see a monster?"

He grabbed her by the hair and dragged her—screaming—into the bedroom. He was strong and drunk and enraged. Her kicking and clawing was no match for his strength and only fueled his fury. He punched her in the stomach, and Patty doubled over. He ripped her shirt off and punched her again. She couldn't breathe. She was terrified. With his belt and her shirt, he tied her legs to the bed frame. Tearing off her sweatpants and holding her down, he had his way with her.

• • • •

Back at the office, William found himself once again working away at his desk in Cubicle 1. He could hear others talking on their telephones or hammering away at their keyboards when his telephone-intercom came to life. "Lancaster." It was the President.

William pushed the speak button: "Yes, sir?"

"Can you join me in my office?"

"Of course, sir," William replied, and he took a quick sip from his coffee, and then with a slightly trembling hand, he set the cup down at its place on his desk. He stood up and straightened his tie. He noticed Mary poking her head up from below her cubicle, and she gave him a smile. Her head quickly retreated back down into her cubicle as Natalie and Nathan popped up, who quickly waved before sinking back down to their own desks. Kind of like moles, William thought. Or prairie dogs. As William stepped out into the aisle, he glanced back toward Nolan's cubicle. Nolan was leaning his head out with a big grin on his face and a "thumbs up" on his hand below it. William smiled back at him, then turned and headed toward the President's office.

Yes, this was it. Anderson was going to tell William how loyal he'd been, how he'd been such a great worker, and it was time for him to move into an office: Office 4. William could hardly keep from smiling, but he knew he needed to keep a professional demeanor, so he fought off the temptation and sat down in the chair across from the President's desk (after he had motioned towards it, of course). Anderson's office space took up the whole end of the building, as well it should. The building was circular on both ends, and so the exterior wall of the President's office was curved. And surrounded almost entirely by windows. (An oval office!) The fountain outside spurted water twenty feet into the air until the water changed direction and splashed lazily back down into the small pond below it. Inside, the room was spacious, and even with the huge wooden desk that faced the interior of the office, there was plenty of room for Anderson to practice his putting (even his free throws if he'd so desired). The desk was spotless and void of any kind of paperwork. (That was why he had William and his coworkers, after all.) A large granite piece of artwork sat in front and center of the desk, a miniature Stonehenge kind of thing, and if William had been much shorter, he would have had to look around it.

"Lancaster." He called everyone by their last name. William heard him close the door behind him, and then Anderson came around his desk and stood behind his chair. The fountain outside framed the President: a moment frozen in time, a picture of absolute beauty. "Lancaster. You are a great asset to this company. You are probably our hardest worker, and your long hours and dedicated service has not gone unnoticed." This script was playing out better than William could have imagined. "Of course you know by now that Tosh is retiring, and his last day is at the end of next week." William nodded. "Which means that it will be necessary for us to implement some changes around here." William continued to nod and continued to suppress the smile that was getting larger and larger inside of him by the moment. "Wilson will be moving into Tosh's office and taking over his key responsibilities. Ms. Rather will fill Wilson's current position and office, and I'm looking forward to seeing all that she does with his old region of the country. That leaves the important position and office that will be vacated by Ms. Rather. You are in line for this promotion, and I'm happy to say that you have earned it and deserve it."

William could not hold in the smile any longer, and he said, "Thank you," as he grinned from ear to ear.

"There is just one problem." William's smile was locked-in, but suddenly felt forced. Did the President just say what William thought he said? "You see, my nephew Christopher has just graduated from Stanford and desperately needs a new job in this ever-expanding medical supply industry. Because he has just finished schooling, he is well aware of the current trends in our industry, and he knows all about the latest and greatest technology that day-by-day is being improved and upgraded. He had impeccable grades and is a real go-getter. I just feel at this time that he might be a better fit for Rather's vacated position, and if I keep you where you are, that will be one less extended training session that will be necessary. And of course, who knows what the future may hold. If someone else leaves or retires, I will move you up to an office position faster than a snap of a finger. I know you're a good company man, and I appreciate your understanding."

William was speechless. A million things were coursing through his brain and he could form none of them into words that he could spit out. This was all wrong! Wilson was the oldest of the group, and he was only forty-seven. He wasn't going anywhere soon. And who would leave a company after just getting a promotion and a better office, better pay, and better benefits? None of the people were going anywhere, and it looked like William wasn't either. This was just plain wrong.

"I'm sure you'll want some time to digest all this, Lancaster. Tomorrow is Friday. Why don't you take tomorrow off—a free vacation day—and the rest of today, for that matter. Have a long weekend to relax and rejuvenate. And remember, I have an open door policy. Please feel free to discuss this matter with me at any time."

William couldn't think of anything to say, except maybe "Bull!" and that just didn't seem like the right thing to say at the time. His mouth was hanging open to his chest, his eyeballs were glazing over, and his brain was fogging up as he turned slowly away from Anderson and moved toward the door. William walked back to his cubicle and turned to look back toward the President's office. Anderson was closing the door and seemed to be averting a look in the direction of the cubicles. William sat in his chair and buried his head in his hands. He normally would have started crying, but at the moment, he just felt numb. The whole thing seemed so surreal—like it hadn't actually happened—but William knew it was real.

Earl Nolan came up behind him and was about to give him a slap on the back when he noticed something was wrong. Nolan's smile instantly disappeared, and he stared for a moment at William, and then he shook his head. William would have heard Nolan say, "Bullshit!" if he had been capable of hearing anything at the moment.

The eagle has fangs
The eagle has claws
Diving in for the kill
The butterfly is helpless

He stumbled out of the bedroom after he had finished. Patty heard the outside door slam. He was gone. She just laid there for a while, the tears streaming down her face. *Is this the only type of treatment I'll ever know? Do I deserve nothing better?*

She untied her feet. *How dare he bind me.* She looked at her shirt—it was ruined. She showered and let the warm water wash over her, draining the violence away as best she could. As hot as she could stand it, the water splashed onto the top of her head, over her face (with the last of the tears), down her body—bruises and all. She used up all the hot water, and after it turned cold, she put on one of Roy's T-shirts and a pair of his boxers. Patty hated the smell of him in the shirt. She hated having to wear his clothes. She hated what he did to her sweatpants and shirt. And she hated she had nowhere to go. But it was too far of a walk to Aunt Meredith's. She had no one else to call. Roy was her whole life. Except for school. What a life. What a sad, miserable life. *Was there nothing more for her?*

TEN

Later that night, Maggie was not speechless when William told her the news just before dinner. William was sitting in his customary spot—head still in his hands—and she was standing by the stove waving a spatula around.

"He what!!?? He can't pass you over. You've been there too long and have put in too many long hours, long days, blood, sweat, and tears. His nephew has to start at the bottom just like everyone else. You need to go in and talk to him and tell him this just isn't right. It isn't fair and it can't work out. And he's acting like he's so nice for giving you tomorrow off. Right! He's just letting you have three days to cool off and not be all huffy and puffy. You got to talk to him, William. What do you think? You can't let this happen. It just isn't right. I want you to get out a piece of paper and start writing down all your thoughts about this: everything that comes to your mind. And then you think them through some more and put them together to present to him. Here's a piece of paper and here's a pencil, William. You got to do this. What are you thinking about? Say something."

William was still numb. He didn't know what to say. And she wasn't helping matters by going into ramrod mode. William needed time to process everything. Maybe having the extra day was a good thing.

"William, are you not going to do anything about this? You should quit, that's it. Call him up and tell him to stick it. You ain't putting up with this. That's what you should do. What do you think? They'll be lost without you, and then they'll come begging you to come back. You can say, 'Only if I get Office 4.' He'll have to agree because the company will not survive if you are not there. You do all the work.

Everybody else is nothing but loafers and slackers. What do you think? You got to put your foot down, William, and get aggressive. This is the perfect time for you to work on your assertiveness. Get right in his face, wag your finger at him, and tell him to stick it. You like that idea better, William? Do you? What are you going to do, William? Talk to me. What can I do to help? What do you want me to do?"

William was about ready to pull his hair out—pull his ears off, actually. She was freaking out and not helping him in the least. William slowly looked up at her and simply said, "shut" followed by "up," and then he went back to putting his head in his hands. He felt like the world was pushing down on the back of his head, and he had to exert all the energy he had to keep his face from smashing down into the table. His head splitting, his neck stiff and sore, and his back was hurting. The pressure was incredibly unbearable, and the noise of her talking was not helping at all. William felt like he was going to explode and pieces of him would land all over the room. He actually thought that this might not be such a bad thing, and he began hoping that he would indeed explode. At least things would be over and done with. He waited. Nothing. Nothing happened at all. Well, except the pot on the stove boiled over, and then William heard the hissing as the liquid ran onto the hot stove, and then he heard uncharacteristically Maggie cursing and scrambling to move the pot, and then burning herself and cursing some more. William laid his head down on the table and remained in that position for what seemed like—and actually was—hours.

· · ·

Roy was drunk and out of his mind. He drove and drove, still drinking from his bottle, not really aware of anything. When he pulled into a gas station off of the interstate, what he did was not premeditated, but it seemed to come naturally.

No one was in the store; only the attendant. Roy had a baseball cap pulled low on his forehead as he set his fresh six-pack on the counter.

"Hey there," the attendant said. "Eight twenty-one."

Roy did not look up. His hand reached into his jacket and he pulled out his handgun. It was an old 22-caliber, but enough to do damage.

Still not looking up, he spoke low and slow. "Give me all the money you got."

"Ok, Ok. We don't keep too much in here though."

"Gimme."

The young man handed him a pile of ones, some fives, a couple of tens, and a twenty. Roy grabbed and flipped through it with one hand.

"There ain't much here."

"I'm sorry."

Roy shook his head. "Shit." Without looking up, he motioned toward the bottles behind the counter. "Give me a fifth of the good stuff."

The attendant handed him a fifth of whiskey. Roy grabbed it, and headed for the door, still keeping his head hung low. He jumped in his car and barreled down the interstate. At the next exit, he got off and crossed back over, and then headed back in the direction he came. That should keep 'em off my back, he thought.

He counted the money. Seventy-nine dollars. He hit the dash. *That ain't shit!*

When he got back to his place, he barely made it in the door before he passed out on the couch. He didn't even know that Patty had barricaded the door to the bedroom. She heard him come in. Heard him snoring almost immediately. And cried herself to sleep.

William slouched in his car. Staring blankly ahead. It was lunchtime. His lunch sat unattended next to him. Lately, he did not feel too friendly at work. Somewhat pissed off and embarrassed, though. So his lunches were now spent alone in the car.

He parked his car at the edge of the lot. Next to it the road continued on about fifty yards and then stopped before a field of weeds. Yellow signs, five of them, blocked the way. The middle sign was larger, diamond-shaped, with the words Dead End displayed on it. William stared at the sign. His eyes didn't even blink.

Dead End. Dead End. Dead End. William Dead End. Dead End William. It was all the same. His job. His wife. His life. The future, even the past. Dead End.

He felt so alone. He felt so detached. In one way, it was almost freeing. He could do anything and to hell with the consequences. What could be worse than his current existence? Nothing. No matter what he did and whatever those actions produced, it could be no worse than the Dead End.

Maybe he should rob a bank. Smoke a bunch of pot. Kidnap a young lady. Kill his wife. Hell, kill everyone inside the building behind him. He could understand the despair that drove people to such acts. He could understand the attraction even. And even though these thoughts should frighten him — before *would* have frightened him — such thoughts now only felt somewhat appealing.

Or maybe he should just leave. Drive to wherever. Start anew. Go to California. Hell, go to Alaska. No one would find him there. Would he still be a nobody there? Dead End William? Probably. That's what made him a Dead End.

Maybe ending it all was the answer. What are the ways to die? Carbon monoxide? A slash of the wrists? A bullet to the head? Maybe even swinging from a rope? No — those would all be painful. Maybe the pain would be intoxicating? Maybe some pain would ease the pain? Nothing eases the pain of a stubbed toe more than conking your head at the same time. One larger pain always overrides a smaller one, right?

William leaned back and then crashed his forehead as hard as he could into the top of the steering wheel. The car rocked. He saw flickering stars. It hurt.

He did it once more. The second time hurt no less. But no more either. Ha! — another Dead End. Pain must not be the answer.

To jump from a tall building. That would at least give you an ending quickly and presumably — painless. And the ride down would be a one-of-a-kind experience. Something very few have had the privilege of experiencing. That fall — the longer the better — must be exhilarating. Yes — leading to the final, complete Dead End.

Dead End William. He got out of his car and went back into work. Lunch break was over.

My own private prison
My own private prison
The door is open
And I can't get out

The next morning, Patty grabbed a ride on the bus to school. Roy wouldn't be budging from his stupor for quite some time. She had guessed if you deserve a good drunk, it's after losing your job. She didn't believe that anymore. And she was still livid at how out of hand he'd gotten. Why do guys turn into such monsters when drunk? Aunt Meredith says there are nice guys out there. Patty had never met one.

School was slow and a blur. She couldn't focus. Patty had tons of makeup on; she had her hair hanging low over her face, so no one really noticed her. No one ever noticed her anyway except for being the stupid girl at Roy's side. She'd thought about trying to make new friends, but she could never bring herself to talk to anyone. Certainly not that day — all banged up. What if they thought she was weird? Besides, everybody had already buddied-up and created their cliques — and they left her out. Alone.

When the dismal dismissal bell rang, she planned on riding the bus to Aunt Meredith's. She'd hoped she would be home (and alone) that night. Aunt Meredith was staying out more and more each week, too. Patty figured Aunt Meredith basically forgot about her, too. Ignored her anyway. What the hell. She was accustomed to that.

But at the edge of the parking lot, there stood Roy — all smiles, looking energized. No sign of a hangover. He was leaning on the hood of his car, and he came toward her when he saw her.

"Patty, please please please forgive me." He pressed his palms together and bowed his head. "I was a total jerk. I deserve your hatred and anger. But that wasn't me last night. You know that."

He looked at her. She was not sure why she stopped to listen. Well, that was a lie. He and his gorgeous blue eyes were all she had — it was pathetic. But she was still plenty pissed off.

"You really hurt me, Roy."

"I know. I know. I want to take it all back and do it over. Better. I want your pain. I deserve it. You deserve nice things." He took her books and gently pulled her elbow toward his car. "I got something nice for you today. Come see."

She went. Reluctantly. But still she went, the loser that she had become.

He put her books in the back seat and grabbed a small bag. He handed it to her. "Open it."

She reached into the bag and within was a small black box. Patty glanced up at Roy—who was smiling now—and then opened the box.

Inside was a delicate blue butterfly on a small gold chain. A beautiful blue stone sat in the middle of the wings.

"That's a blue sapphire," Roy said. "Not a cheap one, either. You deserve the best." He opened the passenger door and helped her sit down, her legs still outside the car. He took the butterfly from the box and knelt in front of her. People were looking at them, but Patty didn't care. Roy dragged her right pant leg up and placed the chain around her ankle. The last time he had touched her ankle, he was tying it to the bed. It was sore to his touch, and she grimaced.

"I am so sorry, Patty. This belongs on your beautiful ankle. And it's a reminder of the meanness I committed to you last night. I'll never do that again. Please forgive me."

He looked up at her and she noticed his eyes matched the color of the sapphire. Damn him—it was hard for her to stay angry at him. "Don't you ever tie my feet again, Roy." Sternly.

"No way, baby. I promise." He stood. "Let's get out of here."

She swung her legs into the car. The anklet sparkled in the sunlight. She had to admit it was beautiful.

•   •   •

An hour later, in his bed, she lay naked except for the anklet under a single sheet. Roy was holding her, caressing her hair, his hard body pressed against hers. He had been so gentle this time—so loving—so tender. They stayed that way for the longest time.

About ten o'clock, Roy slipped out of the bed and put on his jeans. He leaned over and kissed her forehead. Patty had been asleep, and was still half sleeping, barely awake.

"I got to run out for a minute, baby," he said. "You fall back asleep, OK? I'll be back later."

He left the room in the dark. She was back asleep in seconds.

Maggie Lancaster stood at her kitchen window and watched William working in the yard. Her husband loved his yard and took great pride in how immaculate he kept it. Always comparing it to the neighbor's, he'd remark: "I cannot believe that the Peacocks are cutting their yard in a diagonal again. Don't they know it's better to mix up the mowing patterns, not only for the benefit of the grass's health, but for creative variety, too?"

"No one keeps a yard like you, William," she'd reply.

Lately, though, Maggie noticed a harsher edge to William's personality. He was always quiet, but now even more so — as if he had withdrawn entirely within himself. She worried about him. He needed a break. A long one. Maybe a new job entirely? The way they treated him at Anderson Supply, it was no wonder he was on edge.

Maggie tried to console him. She'd talk soothingly to him, give him ideas to be more assertive, more open, and other ways to fit in. But none of the myriad of ideas seemed to sink in. They'd bounce off and land unattended at his feet.

All she wanted was to be there for him; to make things better. If it wasn't for William, she'd be so lonely. She talked to very few other people. Her sister, of course, but with all her kids, she was always on the run. She had no time for Maggie's tea and crumpets. William was Maggie's one and only. Only lately, when he was around, he was so distant — like he was at some other place — far, far away.

She heard the roar of the lawnmower as it kicked to life. At least she had talked him into taking a few days and fishing at her sister's cabin. She was sure it was not long enough of a break, but any little bit was bound to help. Maggie hoped to pander to his every need, and make sure he had some quality downtime doing whatever he wanted — including doing nothing. She had even packed that slinky red nightgown she had bought on a whim a couple of years earlier. Maggie wasn't sure she could still get into it, but you never have those things on for long, anyway. She figured she could hold her breath for that long.

Maggie realized she had a little grin on her face. William looked in on her as he went past, pushing the lawnmower. She waved coyly at him, which caused a confused look on his face, and a near miss with a tree, since he wasn't watching where he was going. He glanced back at her again, this time with an angry look on his face, and she giggled.

PART TWO

ONE

The wind blew through the vinyl sign that hung in front of the country gas station. It gave the prices for a gallon of gas. It rattled and made a flipping noise—threatening to blow over—but the owner had taken assurances (with concrete blocks) that it would take a bigger wind than the one blowing to topple the sign. The sign rat-a-tat-tatted against the wooden pole that held up one side of the roof that protected customers filling their tanks (or the filling station attendant, because this gas station actually still offered full service). The gas station itself was a white (at least at one time) square structure with a porch roof lining the front side. The owner/attendant/mechanic would sit on the wooden bench under the roof most of the day, unless there was a car that needed worked on, gas to be pumped, or something else to take care of inside. There was a two-bay garage in the rear of the building, and on some days there was a car needing a tune-up or brakes or some other ailment fixed. You entered the garage from the east side of the building, and on the west side of the building, a path lead to the house that was situated a hundred yards away. Kennett, who had inherited the house (as well as the gas station), lived there alone, trying to make ends meet as best he could. Kennett was forty-four and both of his parents had died: his father of cancer nine years before, and his mother of a heart attack last February. He moved back into the house at that time and sold the trailer that he used to live in with his wife before the divorce was finalized three years ago. He'd been alone and lonely ever since, and frequently wondered what might have become of Tonya—his ex, who had moved to Louisville, Kentucky with her boyfriend not long ago. He still had affections for her, but he tried not to think of her — although he was unsuccessful on most days when he sat on the bench in front of the gas station.

On this day, a young couple that had pulled in for a "fill up" in an old, beat-up, compact car had distracted him. Kennett got up and stretched, then he shuffled over to the car.

"How you doing?" he asked.

"We'd be doing a lot better if we had gas in our car."

What a smart-aleck punk, Kennett thought. "Regular?"

"Yeah, fill 'er up Ethyl." The punk laughed at his own joke, if that was what you'd call it.

As he got their tank filling, they said they wanted to buy some gum. "Do you carry any gum, Ethyl?" And then laugh again.

Kennett just ignored him. "We got three kinds: Big Red, Juicy Fruit, and CareFree."

The young man, (seventeen? eighteen? nineteen?), had hair that was not long, but it was unkempt and looked like he spent no time on grooming (or bathing). He guessed short Number Four clipper hair helped, because it was hard to mess it up. The woman — girl really, no more than sixteen at the most — was long and thin, with long shoulder length dirty blonde hair. Kennett noticed her pretty green puppy dog eyes right away — these not dolled up with any makeup either. She was somewhat pretty, definitely not homely, but all the more appearing like she could use a good bath, too. Both wore blue jeans with seemingly more holes than fabric (although he had to admit that the young lady filled her jeans very well, and, as they made their way inside, he got caught more than once eyeballing her butt by her boyfriend, who indicated nonverbally that he did not like that one bit). He had on a flannel shirt with the sleeves ripped off. A tattoo of an American flag was on his left bicep. She wore a white T-shirt under a grey windbreaker tied around her waist, and she carried a purse made of blue canvas.

So into the little store they went — which had little more than gum. Some old Hostess pies, cans of oil, old candy bars, maps and brochures, a big cooler full of soda and beer (more flavors of beer than gum, that's for sure), and the gum, of course, in the said three flavors: Big Red, Juicy Fruit and Carefree. Kennett finished with the gasoline and joined them inside, wiping his hands on his rag that he always kept hanging from his belt on his right side.

Kennett went around to the back of the counter—a glass-enclosed thing that housed the various kinds of candy bars and snack cakes (and the gum, of course). The girl leaned over and looked into the counter, and Kennett leaned over and looked at the girl leaning over, and caught a glimpse of cleavage. He glanced up at the man, who stood with his hands on his hips and a snarl on his lips. Kennett decided he better stand up straight, and he did so, wiping his hands on his rag one more time.

"I'd like some Carefree," the girl said, although she appeared as if she was nowhere near being carefree.

The man made his way up to stand next to her, and as Kennett leaned into the display case, the man took the girl's purse. She looked at him funny when he did, and she gasped when he pulled a Smith and Wesson from inside it.

Kennett put his hands (now holding the gum) up in the air. Then he reached out with the gum to the girl, and then he put his hands up again. Finally he gave the girl the gum and said, "No charge, please." Then he put his hands back up in the air for good this time.

"What are you doing, Roy?" the girl said loudly. "Stop it!"

"Yeah, thanks for the gum, dill wad," the man said, ignoring her, "but we want all the money you got in this joint."

"Roy! Stop!" she yelled.

Kennett lowered his hands immediately, but then he realized it might have been too fast, so he kind of started to put them back up again, and then slowly he moved them toward the cash register.

"Yeah, nice and slow would be good," the man with the Smith and Wesson said. "Honey, shut up and go stand over there. You're making me nervous and you don't want to make a man with a gun nervous."

Kennett pressed the button and the cash till slid open.

"I'm not doing this, Roy," she said. "I don't need this gum. Let's just go."

Roy grabbed a hold of the girl by her hair and yanked her head toward him roughly. "Patty," he said through clenched teeth, "take your ass over there by the door and chew your fucking gum. Anything to keep your mouth quiet." Then he kind of flung/threw her by her hair toward that part of the store. She winced and grabbed the back of her head, but she obeyed him this time and went to the door. "Make sure no one comes in, OK?" He said to her, and then he turned back to Kennett. "Come on, where's my money?"

Kennett grabbed all the cash in the till and handed it to Roy. Roy backed up a bit, somewhat stunned, and looked at the cash. "What the hell is that? There's only like one hundred dollars there?"

"One hundred and ten dollars, sir," Kennett added. "It's been a slow day."

"You got to be shitting me. That is all you got?"

Kennett had his hands back up. "Well, sir, the gas station is fairly out of the way from everything, and when I do get car work, you know, a tuneup or mechanic stuff, they usually pay by a check and not cash. You are welcomed to my checks—I have two here—each for a couple of hundred bucks."

Roy looked down and just shook his head. "I don't want your checks, you ass wipe." Suddenly he said *FUCK*, and he got all pissed off and kicked the counter hard with his boot. The counter was more solid than Roy expected, and it hurt his big toe. He said FUCK again, as the girl jumped (and gasped). So did Kennett. But the worse thing was that Roy's Smith and Wesson discharged at the same time. The loud sound in the small place was deafening. The bullet barely missed Kennett's head and smashed into the window, shattering it into pieces. This made Roy even more pissed, and he started to stomp around in there, all the while he kept repeating *Fuck fuck fuck*.

"Patty!" he yelled. "Go grab all the beer you can. Two twelve packs or eighteen packs, or however much you can." She was standing with her hand over her mouth. "Now!" he screamed, and she hustled to the cooler. Roy moved behind the counter and he shoved the barrel of the gun under Kennett's nose. Kennett could feel the heat on the barrel from the fired shot. "Hand me your phone," Roy said. Kennett slowly picked up the phone and gave it to Roy. Roy jerked it out of his hand and smashed it to the floor. Then he tugged on the phone line, yanking it free from the wall. Kennett was hoping Roy didn't check his pocket where he kept his cellphone—that's the phone he always used. Softly, but surely, police squad car sirens could be heard growing in intensity in the distance. Roy said *Fuck* one more time, then he hustled over to the cooler display and grabbed a twelve pack himself.

Patty had moved back by the door, a twelve pack in each hand. "Roy, I can't believe this. We are going to get in so much trouble."

"Shut up! Things will be just fine! GO!"

They exited the little gas station and, after throwing all the beer in the backseat, swiftly jumped into their car. Roy fired the car up. It backfired with a bang, kicked into life, and he slammed it into gear. The tires smoked as he pulled out onto the road, the sound of the sirens growing louder and louder.

"You think that's the cops?" Roy asked.

"Of course it's the cops!" she yelled. "You just shot at a guy in a gas station! Armed robbery, Roy! I can't believe it!"

"OK, OK, calm down," he said.

"Calm down???!!!! You've got to be kidding! I was with you! I'm an accomplice."

"Let me think a minute," he said. The car sailed down the road, but it still seemed like the sirens were getting louder and louder. "I got it. I'm going to pull off up here on this side road."

"That's brilliant, Roy!"

"Shut up! I'm not finished!" he yelled. "I'm going to drop your ass off and you go hide. Then I'm going to go down the road a little ways and then turn around. I'll be headed back to pick you up—the cops will see me going in the other direction—just one guy and not a guy and a girl, if they even know that—but they won't suspect I'm their guy. They'll blast past me going in the other direction, and then I pick you back up and off we go—care free!"

"Yeah, whatever!" she said. "Just let me out of here."

"Hold on. Here's the road. Get ready!" And he took the turn fast, and the car went into a slide. Miraculously, Roy controlled it pretty well, and the car righted itself as it tore down the gravel road. He went a hundred yards down the road and into the thick of the surrounding trees and then slammed on the brakes. "Get out! I'll be back before you know it!"

Patty jumped out of the car and, as soon as her feet hit the ground, headed for the trees. Roy blasted in reverse and turned the car around, then pulled back in the direction from whence he had just came. His idea, as crazy as it was, may have actually worked, except by the time he got turned around and back to the road, the cops were already arriving. Two cars pulled up and blocked the road and three cops were out of their vehicles with their pistols raised in an instant—two officers leaning across the hoods and one pointing over the roof of the second car. A fourth officer remained in one car, in case Roy had ideas of running.

Roy slammed on his brakes and almost collided with one of the cars. He had started to go around, but the ditches on both sides were deep and he never would have made it. The dust from the car enveloped everyone, and for a moment, Patty couldn't see them. But the thick dust cover cleared too quickly, and Roy was only half in and half out of the car. He stared at the three guns pointed at him. Then in his car at his gun. Back at the cops. From inside the second patrol car, an officer yelled through the car's external speaker: "Come out with your hands up! Now!" Roy watched the last of the dust slowly dissipate, and then he slowly got out the rest of the way—his hands raised. Patty saw his lips mouth FUCK one last time.

• • •

It had happened overnight. What had been the best maintained yard in the neighborhood—pristine, green, weedless—had succumbed to a zig-zag of ridges and mounds. Tunnels that must have taken all night to dig. God Forsaken Mole!

William Lancaster's pride and joy was his yard. He lived for his yard. He had little else to live for: an overbearing wife, and an overburdening job, no kids, no hobbies. His grass and yard occupied many—most—hours of his free time. And now it had been invaded by an evil intruder. A rodent.

In the predawn light of a summer day, William sat in a lawn chair looking out over the expanse of his domain. He was out of breath but somewhat satisfied, after having carefully flattened each and every tunnel the mole had made, and, for the moment, his yard was once again flat and immaculate. William knew moles ate breakfast—their favorite meal of the day—and he was going to make best use of this knowledge. He waited. And watched.

The hiss of his neighbor's sprinkler system alerted the world to its coming to life, and William turned to watch the spray rotate around the yard. It better not touch my yard, he thought. He, too, had a sprinkler system, but he had mathematically adjusted his own system to water the lawn in precise increments, and at premium times. Not only a science but also an art.

William turned back to his yard, satisfied that the neighbor's water would stay off of his lawn. He gripped the handles of two shovels, one in each hand, and admired the sun as it appeared on the horizon. It looked to be a beautiful day, perhaps on the warm side, but the early morning temperature was comfortable. He glanced at his cellphone sitting beside him and noted the time. He still had twenty-two minutes before he had to leave for the office. Come on, mole, wake up.

The screen door opened behind him and his wife, Maggie, leaned out. "What are you doing, William? Don't you have to go to work?" She always spoke loud, and it made William start, especially in the stillness of the morning. He turned and frowned at her, and waved her back inside (one shovel falling to the ground), and then put his finger to his lips. "Quiet! Get out of here before you screw it up."

"Why do I have to be quiet? Are you meditating?"

He stood up and stomped (quietly) over to her. "I'm trying to get that mole!" he whispered. "Get back in the house!"

"Oh," she said. "I was wondering. Two shovels. Kind of hard to dig with two shovels at the same time, isn't it?" She giggled, and he pushed her back inside. As he returned to his shovel and chair, he glanced back out at the yard. A slight movement caught his eye about ten yards out. The grass lifted up into a tiny mound, and then slowly spread away from him. *I got you, you little son of a bitch.*

William tip-toed to the location and sunk the first shovel at the beginning edge of the tunnel. Then he shoved the second a foot in front of where the movement was headed. He thought he felt (and heard) a clink. The mole had collided with shovel two. It pained William to flip the sod up in the air—his precious grass—but a furry, dirty, wiggling ball came up with it.

"Hello, Mr. Mole," he said.

Maggie, watching from the door, recoiled a bit as William raised the shovel high in the air, and with all his force, brought the edge down on the furry rodent. It wiggled furiously, and William hacked again at the little creature. Once, twice, three times, four. The wiggling stopped, but William did not—furiously hacking the mole again and again—until it was a bloody mess of fur and claws. William's eyes were wide and his breathing heavy. But then he suddenly stopped, and a smile spread across his face.

. . .

Two of the cops came toward him. One of them held a gun pointed at Roy, while the other one told him to turn around. Roy did so. Then the cop pulled Roy's hands down behind his back—hard and tight—and Roy winced. The handcuffs were on his wrists immediately.

"Where is your girlfriend?" That was the cop who was holding the gun on him.

"I'm all alone," Roy yelled over his shoulders, and then he turned back around to face him.

The other two cops had come up to them by now, and the one motioned to the other that they should head out toward the trees—in Patty's direction—and toward her they came. She realized her hiding spot in the trees was crap, and so she quickly backed through the trees, getting deeper and deeper into the woods. Patty found that the brush and the thickness of the trees got worse and worse, and although it made for better cover, it also made it more difficult to move. She did not think the cops had seen her yet.

After moving forward as quietly as she could, she stopped and peered back from the cover of a large pine tree. The two cops came to the exact spot where she had entered the woods, and they, too, come into the trees at that same location. That made her nervous. Patty turned and moved further on, coming upon a wildlife path. Thankfully, this would make the going easier, but she worried that if the cops found it, they would be able to spot her. So she took off running at full speed when she hit the path and was thankful that the going was at least quiet. It was so quiet that she thought she heard some kind of noise in front of her down the path, and before she could determine what the noise was, she came to the river—flowing freely. Patty was sure that Roy would be getting a ride to the station and would not be coming back to pick her up. She had to get away from the cops or she would find herself sitting next to him in the squad car. It was this thought that propelled her into the water.

TWO

Immediately cold and wet, her clothing ponderous and pulling her down — now completely soaked — very heavy and hard to move in. She must stay in the shallow waters if she did not want to sink below the surface — and as soon as she realized this, she slipped on a slimy rock and went under. The current took her quickly downstream. Oh, it was hard to breathe without getting a mouthful of water. The good news was that she was moving fast and getting away from the cops quickly. The bad news was that she was having a hard time keeping her head above the water. *I'm going to drown — all because of a stupid pack of gum.*

. . .

"If it wasn't for William, I'd be so lonely." Maggie had made her daily call to her sister, Martha.

"Have you thought about joining a group of some kind? Maybe you could meet other women like yourself."

"I've tried all that. The Ladies' Guild at church — a bunch of old ladies knitting. No thanks. And I did that painting class that one time, remember? In the first class, some old guy came in and took off all his clothes. I couldn't paint *that!*"

Her sister giggled. "I remember that! So funny. You said he had wrinkles on top of his wrinkles." She paused. "But what about a book club?"

"Boring."

"Or a Zumba class?"

"Ouch."

"Maggie, you need to get some kind of hobby. And then join a group and make friends."

"Yeah, like, is there a cleaning ladies' club? No—we're too busy cleaning."

"Maggie, you are impossible."

"I'm sorry," she said. "I enjoy hanging around and doing stuff for William. It makes me feel good. It's just lately he's been so distant. The other day he mutilated a mole. He was so angry. It was like he became a totally different person." She paused. "I think he just needs to get away."

"Maggie, you guys can always use our cabin at the lake. We won't be going down for two weeks. You can have it this weekend, next week, next weekend. What do you say?"

"That would be so great. Thank you. I think a week of fishing will do William a wealth of good. I need the old William back."

. . .

Butterfly Butterfly
No flight with watered wings
Butterfly Butterfly
Sinking

Splashing—hands flailing—trying to get a foothold—finding it and then losing it again—Patty went under again and again—must be a way to stop. Corner of her eye and she saw a tree—fallen and crossing halfway across the river. Patty needed to maneuver to her left a couple of feet. Maybe she could get close enough—grab a hold of it. Stop her demise. Splashing, splashing, giving it her all, down under and then up again—she pushed and flipped and fought herself as hard as she could to her left, when suddenly: Bam! Her back slammed into the tree, knocking what little breath she still had out of her. But she had stopped—immediately. Coughing and gagging, Patty flipped over, draping her arms over the top of the tree—her chest now rested on the top of it—trying to get some air into her lungs. They hurt—empty of air. Her back hurt. The current of the river still tried to drag her down, take her under. A snapping turtle, which had been sunning himself at the end of the log, slid off into the water and she saw it no more.

She breathed deep and appreciated the air that went into her lungs. It hurt to breathe, but felt so good at the same time. When she coughed, she spit out water. Patty looked up and saw a bridge—a bridge familiar—and then she recognized it: it was the bridge into town—Jefferson, her hometown. The waters widened just beyond the bridge, and as they did so, she knew the waters became shallow. After getting herself to a normal breathing rate, Patty let loose of the tree and went under again. But soon she hit the shallow water, and she was able to get to her feet. With effort—her clothing clinging to her—dripping, weighing her down, making her move in slow motion—Patty waded to the edge of the river.

She sat down hard upon a rock and took many deep breaths, her lungs wanting every bit of oxygen available. Looking back upstream, she was sure that she had eluded the police by making it the mile or two downstream. Surely they had not followed. Her lungs seemed satisfied, and most of the water had dripped off, so she clambered up the riverbank and onto dry ground. Patty got her bearing and began the walk toward Aunt Meredith's—right down Main Street. Her clothing was no longer dripping when Bob Gordan pulled up next to her. Bob was one of the few people that had ever bothered to talk to her, at least until Roy beat the crap out of him. Poor guy. But most people ignored her. That was OK. She was a loner, so it bothered her little. But as a loner, she was sometimes lonely. So here was Bob. Roy would be furious if he knew Bob stopped to talk with her. But Patty figured Roy had his hands full, and so she was not too worried about it.

"Well, hello sunshine," Bob said through the open passenger window of his late model white Ford F150. "Where are you headed?"

She smiled at him and went to the truck, leaning in on the door. There was little traffic on the road and he had coasted to a stop by the time she reached him. "I am headed to my aunt's house." She looked down at her clothing and pulled her shirt away from her body. It was clinging in all the right (wrong?) places, and it was still soaking wet, and she was cold—so that was embarrassing, if not immodest. The dripping had stopped, at least. Her jacket, which she would have put on, had been tied around her waist. It had disappeared long ago—and was somewhere at the bottom of the river. "I fell in the water upstream. Don't ask."

Bob laughed. "Hmm—I'm dying to hear the story. You want a ride?"

"Sure, if you don't mind your seats getting wet."

"Jump in. They're vinyl and will dry quick enough. Help clean the dust off of them, too."

Patty climbed in and shut the door, and the truck pulled back onto the road. Then Bob quickly pulled back over to the side. "Where are they off to?" he said, as two police cars went flying past, their lights flashing but their sirens off.

She slinked down in the seat slightly and watched the cars go by. She noticed what looked like Roy in the back seat of the first car. The two squad cars turned the corner, and she didn't see them anymore. Bob pulled back onto the road. Patty was really getting cold now that she was sitting in a breezy truck—wet clothes—with the windows down.

"So why are you all wet?" Bob asked.

Patty looked over at him and shook her head.

"OK, I don't care. I don't need to know." Bob paused for a moment. "What about Roy? You still seeing Roy?"

"Yes, I'm still seeing Roy. Although things may change in that regard without a moment's notice."

William stretched before he went outside. It was once again a new day. The sun was peeking out from below the horizon, and he was eager to enjoy the new morning looking across the beautiful expanse that was his backyard—a sea of green—now that he had killed the little rodent. He opened the backdoor and stepped out into the crisp morning air.

What the hell!

His yard was once again torn up with small hills and tunnels crisscrossing his beautiful lawn. Another fucking mole? The two shovels remained leaning up against the house. He grabbed them and stood silently to the side. Watching. Waiting. *Show yourself, you little motherfucker.*

"William, do you want some coffee?"

His head whipped around. "Shh!!! Can't you see the problem here?"

"Oh, I thought you got that little mole yesterday."

"I did, dammit."

"Well, it looks like he has a little friend." Maggie smiled. "Would you like this cup of coffee?"

"I'd like it if you would keep your fucking mouth shut." William sighed. "But, yes, put the coffee over there. Thank you. Sorry. I'm a little perturbed at the moment."

Maggie set the coffee on the picnic table and then stepped back inside. She was silent, somewhat taken aback. She watched from that vantage point.

William scoured the yard for the slightest of movement. Nothing. *Surely he'll come out for breakfast.* Nothing. *Come on, little mole. Let's dance.*

Suddenly, movement halfway across the yard. A little hill/tunnel started growing—moving east toward the sunrise—on the surface of William's beautiful back yard.

William moved quietly, stealthily, to the spot, and planted the shovel in the ground. He heard the "dink" again as it ran into the blade, then he buried the second shovel behind the little critter. He flipped the sod up and out popped the varmint. Hell, William thought, I'm getting pretty good at this.

The mole started flopping around on the ground. It couldn't see anything—only knew that it was out of the warmth of its little tunnel—out of its element.

William crashed down with both hands on the shovel.

"Take that, you little motherfucker."

He struck down again.

"And that."

Again and again.

"That and that and that."

Again, a squished mess of fur and blood stuck to the end of the blade. William kept pounding.

"Leave my yard alone, you little motherfucker!"

Maggie watched from inside. For once, she didn't say a word.

Aunt Meredith knew better than to ask Patty questions when it came to her relationship and goings-on with Roy. Accepting her back into her home, once again, which she would always do, was pleasure enough—anything to keep Patty separated from Roy, and especially from staying at his place. His place was not in the best part of town, and she assumed it was a dump—judging by the upkeep of himself and his car. When she learned Roy had been picked up and arrested for robbing the gas station, she hoped that Patty's stay may be extended this time.

Armed robbery and firing a weapon: things were not looking too good for Roy. The gas station owner Kennett had only wanted to press charges against Roy. He said he could tell that the girl was there against her will, even though she had taken part somewhat. That, and the fact that she slipped through the cop's hands—well, everyone figured it was Patty—who else would it be? But the cops did not pursue any of those leads—yet—and so she remained in the house of Aunt Meredith's with no visits from the police.

Roy was the older bad boy type, and Patty was attracted to that for some reason—probably the same reason as her mother always was, too—bad choices. Heredity. Could be a father figure for her, Aunt Meredith probably thought, since her father John (The Monster) was a bad boy himself, a heavy drinker, absentee, and moved from one job to another (or not) most of his life. It was what Patty was accustomed to, and so she found herself moving right into a similar relationship.

Bad choices.

"Do you think maybe a few days off would do you some good?" Maggie asked that night over dinner. "A little R and R? Just the two of us?"

William stabbed at the noodles on his plate. A little R and R with Maggie might be the last thing he wanted to do. He looked at Maggie and said nothing. He rarely said anything most of the time. Maggie talked enough for both of them. Hell, Maggie talked enough for an entire football team.

"You know I can ask my sister if we can use her place at the Lake." For some reason, she didn't want to admit that she already had permission. "You've always enjoyed going there and fishing and swimming and barbequing and doing all that fun stuff. It would do you good to get away from the office and all the stuff there you've had to deal with lately. They don't appreciate you one bit. But at the Lake you could have some peace and quiet. Just sit around and listen to the crickets go at it." A giggle. "And listen to the fish jumping — right into the boat and onto the grill. What do you think? Should I ask her? Shoot, it would do me some good, too."

Silence from William, and only briefly from Maggie.

"I'll call her as soon as I do the dishes and see if we can use the place this weekend, and then the following week, too. Maybe even the next weekend, too, but they usually go down at least every other weekend, so I doubt if it would be available two weekends in a row. I guess we could stay there when they are there, too (and here William looked at Maggie and glared), but the kids get on your nerves. And you've been on edge quite a bit lately. Finish your noodles, and I'll call my sister. I think it's a good idea. OK, then it's settled." Psyche him out with the possibility of kids being there, and then tell him it would just be the two of them for ten days or so. She knew how to work him. She knew how to lie — well, not tell him the whole story. Like she already had everything set up. She smiled, thinking about the nice little vacation for the two of them.

• • •

The eagle caressed the butterfly
The butterfly melts
Hiding in his wings
Is peace.

A week later, after they (Roy?) robbed Kennett's service station, the news report said there had been a string of gas station robberies. That had been the fourth one in ten days. They were bringing in witnesses to identify Roy so they could pin them all on him. It didn't look good for Roy. It didn't look like Roy would be coming home for a while. Patty didn't expect to see him again for a long time. And she knew she was right.

She rested, her eyes wide, in a different bed. This one in Aunt Meredith's place. The house was quiet. She was at work. Patty was alone again. There had to be a better life out there for her. She wanted a normal life. She really did. Whatever that was. Patty had never known one. *Will I ever know one?*

Her one escape was her poetry.

. . .

Maggie thinks rest and relaxation will do me some good. There's no hope. I'm beyond that. Life has closed in so tight I can't breathe. There's nothing left to do but explode — to bust the claustrophobic bindings that life has around me. Get rid of my job. Get rid of my house. Get rid of my wife. A clean start. That is the only way. Become someone else. William becomes Bill. A new man. Clean slate. Blank canvas.

That's what was going through William's mind as he stared at the spider spinning a web across the window as he peered out. It slowly went from one side to the other — leaving a web following in its path. Leaving a little bit of itself behind to trap whomever may follow behind. William knew a spider always left a web trail wherever it went. He'd heard this once and had tested it on many occasions. It was easy. Let a spider walk across a pen or pencil, and then lift the pencil. The spider will hang from the pencil because it left its web behind as it crossed the pencil. The test has never failed. A spider was always leaving a web. He needed to be like a spider and be ready to catch whatever it was that followed behind him.

THREE

Patty hated visiting the prison. Every guy she came into contact with ogled her and she felt naked walking through the place with all those eyes on her. Even the guards—they were no better. They would stare at her chest as she walked toward them, and after she passed, when she turned around quickly, the guards and the prisoners were checking out her butt. With no subtlety, or shame, for that matter. Patty could surely understand why, but it sure made her feel like a piece of meat—like she was walking around naked. And to make matters worse, some of the guys even said anything they wanted: *nice ass, baby! Show me your tits!* All the way to *Come on, honey. Let's fuck.* It was disgusting.

And Roy wasn't much better.

"Hey, baby." He was sitting across from her behind the glass. His eyes went from her eyes to her chest, then back to her eyes, then back to her chest. "Can I see your tits, baby?"

She actually thought about it out of pity—for a second, but then she said, "You can go to hell."

Of course, there wasn't much else to talk about. He did nothing except work out in the gym, work in the laundry room, and keep from getting butt-fucked. Patty was not sure how entirely successful he had been in that regard. But she didn't know how many times, or how frequently. She hoped it wasn't a daily—or more—ritual. She didn't know, but she did know that he would NOT talk about it, so if, when, and how many times it happened, she did not know.

Roy frowned and looked back into her eyes. "What have you been up to? Not messing around with any guys, are you?"

"No, Roy. Pretty much just working at Big Mart every night after school. I'm thinking about going to Wild Woods Community College as well."

"Taking poetry shit?"

Oh, he liked to push her buttons. "No, Roy. That's just a hobby. I'm sure I'll end up a secretary."

"Working for some asshole who only wants to fuck you."

Another button pushed. "No shame in working as a secretary."

Roy sneered, rolled his eyes, and then softened a bit. "If you could be anything you want, what would it be?"

Wow—actually a caring question. "You know, there is nothing I'd like better than to be a travel writer. Visit places all over the world and write about what I see and find."

"Good luck with that."

Patty looked at the clock; glad that visiting time was almost over. These visits were never pleasant, and she didn't really know why she continued. Probably wouldn't for too much longer.

"Who works with you at Big Mart?"

"Mrs. Green is my boss. She's nice enough. And another of the girls is Taylor Nash."

"I remember her. What's her ass look like these days?"

Patty just shook her head. The conversation threads were the same at each visit. Dead ends into someone's ass or her breasts. Unless she mentioned some guy, and then Roy would just lose his temper and rant and rave and accuse her of having sex with the guy. So Patty learned after a couple of these visits to never again bring up a guy's name.

She went every week for a couple of months, and then once a month, and by the end of that first year, she had pretty much stopped going. She felt kind of bad about it, but then realized she had a life to live and had to get on with it, as bad as it was. They sentenced him to ten years. *That* was a long time, and she would be old by the time he got out: twenty-eight. They had promised that he might get out in seven years if he behaved well, but she had never known Roy to behave, so she wasn't counting on that.

• • •

Maggie thought she finally had William's attention.

"I talked to my sister, and everything is set. Aren't you excited? One whole week—no, nine whole days of getting away from it all! Just you and me. And the fishes, of course, we can't forget the fishes that you are going to catch. I'll take along a bunch of burgers and hot dogs, but we probably will end up throwing them all away, because you'll be catching so many and such large fish that we will be eating fish until they come out of our gills." Maggie laughed at this. William did not. He just glanced at her. "You know, William, it will do you a ton of good. I saw you the other day when you caught that mole. You beat the living crap out of it. Now I understand you were ticked. Even so, that little guy never saw it coming. This week will do you a bunch of good. The old William will be back. I'm sure of it."

Maggie did not really like this new William. It was still William, but this William seemed so cold, and way more distant. The old William may have been cold and sarcastic, but you could at least hold a conversation with him, and get some kind of response other than "ugh," or "uh," or "um." The old William would surely return after a few days of rest and relaxation. Chillaxing was just what the doctor (and Maggie) ordered.

.   .   .

Everyone called him RoyBoy—but not to his face. Those were fighting words to Roy, even a place as tough as the penitentiary. He would hear those words and instant blind rage. Fists swinging. It didn't matter to Roy if the name-caller was big or small. The only difference was the outcome. Either the name-caller landed in the infirmary—or Roy did. The big guys hit back hard.

He came to be known as RoyBoy after he had become friends with Bruce McGough, a large inmate who weighed in at 300 pounds— mostly muscle. Bruce provided Roy with protection from the other inmates. Of course, the payment for such protection was letting him have his way with Roy, so exactly what he was being protected from Roy sometimes wondered. He guessed it was better to have to do it with just one person than to have to do it all the time with many different people. Ricky Winters had to do that, and it got so bad that he was having to do it more than once a day—one time as many as five times in one day. Afterwards, Ricky couldn't sit for days. So yeah, Roy figured it was better to do things this way. But immediately others started to call him Bruce's Boy, and after a while, it changed permanently to RoyBoy. Roy hated it—a reminder of how fucked-up his life had become.

So far Roy had been locked up for two years. Two long years. Nothing to do. He didn't like sports, so basketball or whatever nonsense was going on at the time was out of the question. And he damn sure didn't want to better himself with more education. He hated school on the outside—hated it more in there. He worked out in the gym some times. And they made him work in the laundry room for a couple of hours every day. Otherwise, nothing to do but sit around. And fume.

Patty, his girl, used to visit all the time in the beginning. For the first couple of months, she came every week when visiting was allowed. Then she got that fucking job at Big Mart and she started to miss here and there. Next came night school for her, and she came even less and less. Fucking bitch. All that he'd done for her and she was letting him rot in the pen. He'd sure let her know about it the next time she visited.

.   .   .

William had not seen any more moles. That was a good thing. Although he had to admit to himself that butchering the little critters felt pretty damn good. Another little guy would probably feel good, too. Getting rid of the uglies in life was very satisfying. And getting rid of them made them memorable. Made them special. Made a life event of getting rid of them.

He was determined to rid his life of all the uglies.

"Long time no see, Patty."

"Sorry, Roy. I've been really busy with work and school and stuff."

They had actually been allowed to sit in the same room together. No glass anymore.

"Yeah, well, I haven't been busy. I sit around here with nothing to do all day. Wait to see you. Wait on visiting days to hear my name called that someone—you—is here to see me. But no!—that hardly ever happens anymore."

"I'm sorry, Roy."

"Listen, Patty. You need to come and see me. Every chance you can! Got it!" He was getting loud, and the guards started to watch him. "I'm rotting in this place and you don't even care!" He went to grab her elbow, but then quickly stopped when a guard made a move toward them. Roy raised his hands up. "Not touching her! Not touching her," he said.

The guard was there. Patty obviously shaken. "Miss, I think it's time for you to go."

Patty got up.

"Wait a minute!" Roy said. "I didn't touch her. Visiting time isn't over yet!"

"Let's go, miss," the guard said, and she followed him toward the check-out point.

"Bullshit," Roy said under his breath. He slumped back in the chair and crossed his arms. He knew if he created even more of a scene, things would only be worse for him. So he sat and fumed.

Patty had not returned. She hadn't been around for three months and four days. He had thought she loved him. Fucking bitch. He tried writing a letter once, but that went nowhere—except a pile of crumpled papers on the cell floor.

Eight more years of this place. He'd go crazy before that.

• • •

Maggie whistled—sort of (she wasn't much of a whistler)—as she straightened up around the house. The sun was streaming in through the windows, and she had a smile on her face.

Vacation time loomed. One week—no nine days—of time at the lake. Just her and William. It was going to be great. She had enough burgers and hot dogs to feed a football team—and a hungry one at that, but she sure didn't want to run out. Plenty of beer, wine, and even two bottles of whiskey. Why not? Maybe they'd be frisky. (Hoped so!)

The bag of marshmallows, chocolates, and graham crackers would be a Saturday evening surprise (along with the new little nightie—accent on "little"—hidden for now in the back of her underwear drawer.)

Maggie's little grin had grown, and she hadn't even realized it. She wouldn't have cared much, anyway.

William wasn't smiling about going away for the week. He had taken time off from work. They didn't care. The bosses were actually being evasive with William, and he kind of liked it. Even so, work had become a major ugly for him. He was not planning on returning. Forever. He had enough money saved up, and he knew he could disappear for quite a while. Long enough to start a new life with a new job and identity.

No more uglies.

He thought that would make a great bumper sticker, but maybe too obvious.

Death to uglies.

That was even better.

Now William smiled. Something, he realized, he had not done for some time.

* * *

Roy got the news that he was being transferred to a different prison facility on a Friday. They never give you any warning, and you have to leave immediately. Of course, it's not like you needed to have time to pack all your possessions for a moving van. Roy owned only a couple of dirty magazines. That was it. He'd get new bathroom stuff and a new uniform at the new place—unknown at this point. His destination would remain unknown until arrival. He'd only moved once before, and that was early on when he left the county prison for the state penitentiary. He actually was looking forward to this move. Roy welcomed any deviation from the norm.

They shackled his legs, fitted with a chain leading to his handcuffs. No chance of running without getting shot.

He climbed into the large passenger van. It had two front seats and three rows of bench seats. One by one, the guards led the inmates into the van: Roy, first, was seated in the back bench seat; a guy named Craig had the middle one; and Terrell sat on the front bench. One guard drove and one guard rode shotgun—with a shotgun. (Is this where the term comes from?)

Down the highway. Nighttime. Past ten o'clock. Little traffic and little else to see except the many lighted billboards. It seemed half of them said *Meramec Caverns*. Some kind of campground with a cave famous for being the onetime hideout of outlaw Jesse James.

Roy didn't really want to sleep, but the darkness, the rumble of the tires on the interstate, and the monotony made it hard to keep his eyes open. Then Craig started snoring. That was enough to keep any guy awake. Roy kicked the seatback in front of him. Craig stirred a bit, and the snoring stopped.

"Hey man. You woke me up."

"No talking back there," said Shotgun immediately.

Craig shook his head, and then he shifted a little. His head fell to the left again, and Roy figured he'd be snoring again soon. Roy watched as a semi-truck passed by. Nothing much else on the road except semi-trucks—and not too many of them. It was a sleepy kind of night.

Suddenly, the tires squealed, and the van jerked toward the shoulder. Roy's head slammed into the window, and as he looked forward, all he could see were bright lights shining in his eyes. Two large white ones and several yellow ones. It was all in an instant.

And then a loud crash.

Roy landed in the grass at the side of the highway. Still buckled to the seat. Along with the last four feet of the van. It was an extended van, and he sat in the extension, alone, slightly below the shoulder of the highway.

His whole body ached. He was dazed. *What the fuck?*

The front portion of the van had disappeared. All he could see was crushed metal under the front end of a semi-truck, still rolling, until it crashed into some trees down the ravine.

Then it was eerily quiet.

.   .   .

Maggie's large suitcase lay open on the bed. It was doubtful whether she would be able to close it, having packed it full of almost her entire wardrobe. She had a second, smaller suitcase opened next to it, and she was filling it with her dailies: socks, underwear, bras. Maggie knew the cabin had a wash machine, but who really wants to do laundry on vacation? She believed in being ready for any kind of hot or cold spell, any kind of function that might come up (a special dance down the road?), or any visitors that might show up. You name it. It was always better to have and not need than to need and not have. William had taught her that, and she thought it wise advice.

Then she thought about what they may need as far as appliances and other household gadgets...

FOUR

In the darkness of night
Swirling lights of red and blue
Screaming noise of sirens, too
The butterfly with no place to land
Flies away — southerly, easterly
Seeking nothing more than peace.

"If you look at my right hand inside my jacket, you'll see I have a gun pointing at you."

Patty could not help but look to where the stranger had indicated. Yep—sure enough. Some kind of hand gun pointed back at her, but barely visible from inside his jacket, the jacket as grungy as the man wearing it. Blue jeans soiled and ratty. An old beat-up baseball cap on his head—it too covered in filth and dirt.

"Yes, it is loaded," he said. "Yes, I have shot it before. Yes, I'm willing to shoot it again." Her eyes looked into his: sunken, sad, detached, while also angry, intense, serious, and somehow familiar. She wasn't sure where she may have seen him before, but she knew she had. Stubble on his face. His left cheek twitched, non-rhythmically, but constantly. "Since you've been so kind to open your cash drawer, I need you to take all the bills and put them into a bag, along with my candy bar, of course."

Out if habit, Patty asked, "Paper or plastic?"

He actually chuckled for a second before replying, "Plastic is fine."

Patty was working check-out lane four in the Big Mart store—a grocery store in the small Missouri town of Jefferson that also sold hardware, toys, books, and auto supplies. No one waited in line behind the man, and no one else worked at any of the other check-out lanes. It was 9:50 p.m. and a customer at this hour would normally have been her last customer of the day. Store closes at ten. Only a couple of other workers were in the store—in the back—and no other customers in sight.

"You're young. You're scared," he said. "Just do what I say and I'll disappear."

Yes—that's all she wanted—for him to disappear. Big Mart's training told her to do whatever an armed perpetrator asked, and the gun pointed at her told her the same thing. Big Mart had no alarm button in place at the register, but Patty knew that Officer House typically drove the parking lot as a courtesy check-up around closing time. At this thought, she noticed headlights pulling into the lot and wondered if it was him.

As she pulled the bills out of the cash drawer and placed them in the bag, the guy showed his first sign of nervousness. "Hurry up, will you?" he said. Then a couple of more left cheek twitches.

Just as she was handing over the bag (plastic) Mrs. Green came around Aisle One. Oh no. She was the manager and said, "Almost closing time." Patty nodded as the man took the bag. He darted for the exit.

"Patty," Mrs. Green said, "you didn't close out his purchase."

Patty nodded again and then toward the man. He stopped momentarily at the door, half in and half out, and glanced back. At the same time, the car outside came to a stop. And yes, it was a patrol car. Hello, Officer House. Bad timing on the perp's part.

When the robber turned back around, he found himself staring at the patrol car. He stopped short. For a second, he froze, but then he pulled out his gun. His first shot exploded and the window of the patrol car shattered. The man took off running across the lot as Officer House rolled out of his car. He fell to the ground, grunting, but quickly regained his footing. Over the hood of his car, he fired his first shot of the night. The man went down, and as he struggled back to his feet, Officer House yelled, "Stop right there!"

Not listening, the man fired again, this time behind himself, back toward the patrol car, as he ran further into the night. The shot went wide and a large pane of glass at the front of the store disintegrated into a million pieces across the floor in front of Patty and Mrs. Green. Office House returned two shots, and the man went down again—no longer struggling—barely moving.

Time stood still. The smoke from Officer House's gun floated away. The coolness of the night filtered in through the shot-out window, and they could hear the buzzing noise from the parking lot lights. Officer House did not move from his perch across the hood, but watched and waited. Mrs. Green stood with her mouth hanging open, and Patty noticed her face nearing the color of her name. Patty exhaled for the first time since the man had stepped outside.

The perpetrator wasn't dead, but he was hurting. The first shot had hit him in the left leg. And one of the second two had clipped him on the shoulder. He squirmed on the ground, the object of his desire—the money bag—out of reach an arm's length away. His gun remained in his hand.

"I got a bead on you, buddy," Officer House said as he stood—slowly and cautiously—from behind the car. "Set the gun down and slowly push it away."

The perp moaned, and the gun clinked as it came to rest on the pavement. He pushed at it, but it only spun—once, twice, stopping—and it was now pointing back at himself.

Officer House crept forward—one step, two steps, three. And he kicked the gun away. "Don't move," he said. "I've still got you in my sights." Officer House backed up to his car for the needed support. He leaned on it, his shoulder bleeding from a gunshot wound, too, and the shattered glass had left multiple cuts on his face and neck. "Hello base," he said into the radio clipped at his shoulder. "This is Car 3 requesting backup and paramedics at Big Mart."

Mrs. Green and Patty moved to the door, each to one side and leaning around to look outside, their faces peeking out from each side of the door frame.

"Stay inside, ladies," the officer said. "Help is on the way." And in the distance could be heard the growing sounds of sirens.

"Shit, Maggie, how you going to close those things?" William asked. Her two suitcases were overflowing.

"Maybe I'll sit on them, smarty pants."

William nodded. "That might work."

She gave him a playful shove on the shoulder. "You didn't have to agree."

William grabbed his suitcase to pack. It was a little brown number. He didn't really think he'd need too much, since he was planning on being there only a day or two. A new start meant new clothes, and what does a guy really need? A couple of jeans and T-shirts. About it, he figured.

He didn't need all this other crap, but he thought for appearances he'd bring a swimsuit and flip-flops. And his favorite beach towel: a large sun setting over the ocean. He used to wear it as a cape and run around yelling, "I am Captain Sun!" Maggie always laughed, but the gag now seemed old and tired.

· · ·

"It was all so loud," Patty said. "First the gunshots, then the sirens. One ambulance came, then another patrol car. Followed by the fire truck. Flashing lights everywhere—all moving in different directions. And all in a different rhythm. With beautiful stars splashed all across the clear sky. Very surreal." Patty sat at the kitchen table with Aunt Meredith. It was now midnight, but the events of the last two hours created a mishmash full of emotions, audio and visual stimuli, and a confusion of what it all meant.

The town of Jefferson was usually quiet, making this evening's events even more disturbing. Since news spreads fast in a small town, Aunt Meredith had heard about the robbery and shoot out by ten-thirty—worried that Patty may be hurt. Her cellphone, stashed away in her purse in the employee break room, went to voicemail eight times—each time Aunt Meredith had called. Finally, on Patty's drive home, she could call to tell her she was fine.

Now they sat together, sipping tea, trying to understand what all had happened.

"He shot at Officer House, and Officer House shot back. It was so loud. And one of the bullets smashed a storefront window as it came in. Lucky we didn't get hit by it, or the broken glass. Who knows where it ended up—probably somewhere in the ceiling." A funny thought hit her. "Maybe it hit a package of toilet paper or something, and a customer will buy it, and then one day they'll find this bullet as they pull out some toilet paper. That would be a shocker." They both giggled a bit. "Officer House got grazed in the shoulder. He'll be OK, although he said it hurt like hell."

"I guess so," Aunt Meredith said.

"I found out the robber is Mike Pretzlode. He's a couple of years older than me, but I remember him from high school. Everybody called him Pretzel. He's shot up pretty bad, but nothing vital was hit. Hospital for him—and then jail. He looked different. I think he's been on drugs for some time." Patty paused for a second, remembering how he used to be in school. "He was a big football star in school. Running back. What a waste."

Aunt Meredith shook her head. "I can't believe he pointed a gun at you."

"He was messed up on meth, I think. He didn't recognize me."

Patty wondered which was better: to be in front of the gun, or behind it. She'd been in both spots now, and they both were unnerving. The other time Patty had not been holding the gun, but still she was on the wrong side of it for sure. Heading down a dead-end path. Not able to stop. Not able to turn around.

Two years had passed since she'd been behind the gun. A lot had changed, but then again, so much was still the same. All she really wanted was to make a better life for herself—but plans always seemed to end up empty. She was still lonely, but enjoyed talking with Mrs. Green at Big Mart. Still bored. It was a simple life. Too simple. The job at Big Mart helped. And night school. Or as most people called it: secretarial school. Not really what she wanted, but could she really expect to be a travel writer? She couldn't even get out of Jefferson. Work Dinner School Read Dream of a Better Life. Repeat repeat repeat. Her poetry at least helped her escape and get away. As did the romance novels she read, of course. Go to other places. Escape to a land all her own.

She wasn't asking for much. But it seemed life—and all those others in it—kept dragging her down and further away from where she'd like to be. What could she do?

Maggie found a couple of canvas bags in the basement. She needed more space to pack things. She still had to pack her bathroom stuff, plus all her beach items—and you never know, there could be a cold night—so a long sleeve blouse, slacks, and a jacket had to go, too. William had finished with his little suitcase long ago. She mentioned having what you might need, and needing what you don't have. He just shrugged and said, "Whatever." And then walked out of the bedroom.

Then Maggie realized she had packed no rain gear yet. Maybe she'd start using large, empty, cardboard boxes to pack stuff, too. They had plenty of those in the basement, she remembered. She headed in that direction. *I know we have at least five or six of those boxes*, she thought.

The shell of the cocoon
So dark inside
But awakening Awakening
It splits and falls away
Butterfly now outside
Somehow still darkness darkness

Roy was in shock. He was moving in auto pilot as he unbuckled himself from the seat, falling further down the embankment at the side of the road. Roy got up and raced toward the cover of the trees. He was in the middle of Nowhere, U.S.A.

Another semi-truck roared by on the highway above, and it occurred to Roy that the crashed semi and van were not easily seen from the road. It was too dark, and the lights had immediately gone out on the van and the semi-truck. The engines were dead. Every piece of wreckage appeared to be down the hill, away from the pavement.

There was smoke lifting, but it was hard to see in the night. And could be mistaken for fog. Dark and quiet. Everywhere.

He moved into the woods—basically blind—with little light from the moon. Onward. Falling. Up again. Tripping over a log. Tripping over the shackles. But still moving. Onward.

• • •

The old William was dead. He had to be, or William could not go on. He could not resign himself to this: rotting in Cubicle 1—forever and ever. One more piece of the mess his life was turning out to be. There were other pieces, of course. Things like their big plans of starting a family right after marriage. That had not happened, and according to all the doctors, never would. It seemed William was just not daddy material. And it probably was just as well. With a dead-end job, how could they ever afford little mouths to feed, not to mention all the medical bills, schoolbooks, and all the toys toys toys? And it sure didn't help one bit that Maggie's sister Martha has been spitting out the kids for ten years. They now had five kids, and William and Maggie assumed they were done. William and Maggie got to be aunt and uncle—whoopee!—whenever Martha and Larry needed a break (or a date). It bugged the heck out of Maggie that her sister had all these kids and she had none, and William got to hear about it all the time—all the time.

"William, wouldn't it have been nice if we had a kid or two? I know you can't help it, but it just isn't the same as watching someone else's kids. Don't get me wrong, I love Margie, Monica, Mark, Mike and Mallory, but having a little Marsha or Mitch of our own sure would be nice. What do you think? Sometimes I wonder if we should adopt, but then the nieces and nephews come over, and that's about all you can handle for a month or two. I guess you don't want to talk about adopting again. Well, that's OK. I'm kind of used to the way things turned out—our lot in life, you know? What do you think? Do Martha's kids really get on your nerves that much? You act like it sometimes, and then sometimes you don't say a word. Well, you never say a word to begin with, but sometimes you act like you actually like them. Is that true? Do you really have a soft spot in your heart for them? At least Mike, I think. You seem to do stuff with him sometimes. He likes to fish like you, so you guys have that in common, anyway. What do you think? You do have a soft spot for Mike, don't you, William?"

She'd go on and on and on and on. And truth be told, William would just as soon never see those kids ever again. He'd like to just crawl up inside a hole and disappear. Like a mole. That way, all the crap would disappear. No more pressure. No more troubles. No more problems. No more pounding! POUNDING! POUNDING! The way things had turned out—well, just give him a hole to crawl inside. Dead-end job, no kids, loud wife, losing his hair, gaining a waist. The old car needed new tires (at least it'd been running that week...), and he was getting old. No wonder he hated his life and blamed his wife. What else could he do but bottle it up and to keep on going.

When he came out of the woods, Roy was in front of a small farmhouse. A barn was out back, and cornfields covered the rest of the landscape. One lone bulb shone from a pole between the house and barn, but inside all was dark.

Roy went around the back of the house. Of course, the door was locked. He started yanking on the door—trying to get it to budge—but nothing. He went to the side window—cursing the jingle-jangle of the shackles and chain. Then a light came on inside. Roy froze next to the door, but went behind a bush, his back to the wall. The back porch light flickered on and out stepped an old guy in a bathrobe.

"Who's out here?" the man said. Roy noticed a pistol in one hand and a flashlight in the other. "Somebody out here?" The man stopped in front of the bush, his back to Roy.

"Just me," Roy said. And as the man began to turn, Roy came down with his handcuffs as hard as he could.

The man went down. The flashlight tumbled away. Roy jumped on his back and hit down again and again.

The man stopped moving after three hits. Roy stopped after seven. He grabbed the pistol from the man's hand, then retrieved the flashlight. He shined the light on the man, and his head was wet, soaked with blood. Roy considered a bullet to his head, but didn't want to risk the noise. The old guy looked dead, anyway.

Roy ventured inside. It was quiet.

"Hello! Anyone here?"

He didn't expect an answer and didn't get one. Searching through the house didn't take long, as small as it was. There was only the kitchen, dining area, living room, and two bedrooms. One bedroom was vacant, and the other had evidence of only one person recently sleeping in it—the sheets having been tossed off in a hurry. The old guy lived alone. (Died alone?)

Outside, the man had not moved. In the barn was a workbench full of tools: saws, grinder, everything Roy needed.

The old small truck with Schrader Farms painted on the side ran pretty rough. It coughed and backfired upon starting, and smoke poured out of the exhaust as Roy pulled down the gravel drive—back toward the interstate.

The old white Ford came equipped with quite a large trunk. With the spare tire correctly put away under the flooring, they could stow suitcase upon suitcase in there. And it was a good thing, too. William Lancaster found himself loading the trunk with suitcases, bags of groceries, more suitcases, boxes of appliances, and still more boxes with more clothes. The suitcases and boxes, seven in all, were not his, save for one of the suitcases—the small brown number. It was the week of their little getaway.

Maggie the Wife stood off to the side of the car with her arms folded, not helping in the least bit, unless, of course, giving directions and talking incessantly about nothing could be considered helping. Along with her lips, her dark black hair was flapping in the wind. She had steadily gained weight since high school, and was plump but pretty. William only wished that most of that weight had not settled in her buttocks. Maggie had managed to keep the ten or fifteen pounds off (New Year resolution) she'd lost at the start of the year, and at five foot four, she carried her plumpness well enough. Come to think of it, he still got a tingle up his spine whenever he caught sight of her beauty mark, a red star-shaped spot that peeked up out of the back of her pants if she bent over too far. Shining five inches above the crack of her ass at the base of her spine. Twinkle twinkle.

William had no room to talk. He had gained twenty-five pounds himself and lost half of that (so it seemed) in hair. The baldness only made his six foot two frame seem all the taller, and thus thinner, which wasn't bad (well, except for the baldness).

Alas, he had agreed to take this trip in a moment of softness (or temporary insanity). Maggie loved to go "out of town," but only if she could pack the entire town with her, plus all the modern conveniences known to humanity. William had plans other than just fishing, so he had only packed a pair of jeans, a couple of T-shirts and his tackle box. Besides a toothbrush, what more do you need?

On and on she droned—in her normal monotone voice. "I got Tommy the neighbor boy to come over and get the mail and paper in for us, and I've left the bathroom window cracked open and the A/C turned way up, so it shouldn't click on, unless it gets to a hundred or something—but it's not supposed to. Dave-on-the-TV said it might rain—fifty-fifty chance, he said, but it shouldn't get above ninety. Boy, I hope not—the cabin's not air-conditioned. Of course, if it does rain, it might cool things down, unless, of course, it drives the humidity through the ceiling. Have you heard anything? I guess if it gets real hot, we'll just end up in the lake the whole time—just to keep cool. What do you think? Do you think we should leave another light on besides the kitchen light? I told Tommy to keep an eye on the place. I bet he comes over with all his buddies and hangs out on our porch. What do you think? I guess that's OK, as long as he doesn't burn the place down with all his cigarettes, but at least that way nobody will rob the place; unless it's Tommy himself, of course."

William slammed the trunk lid down. Hard. "Nobody could steal anything, honey. Everything we own is in the trunk."

"Oh, ain't you just funny?" she said as she jumped in the front seat. His door slammed shut at the same time. He shifted into *drive* and pulled out onto the road.

"Do you think we ought to stop and get some bait somewhere?" Maggie asked. "Maybe some minnows or some worms? I guess you could dig up some worms yourself, huh? That would save us a couple of bucks and they'd be bigger, too — those worms you get at the bait store always seem so little. You know what they say, 'the bigger the bait, the bigger the fish.' You told me that. Didn't you tell me that, William? Anyway, I kind of like minnows though — they don't have that worm junk all over them." She giggled. "Of course not, because they're minnows, not worms, right?" William shot a glance at her without a smile. She smiled back anyway and then turned to look out the window. "Minnows are better for bass, too. Didn't you tell me that — that minnows are better for bass? Let's get some minnows." She turned back. "OK, William?" He simply nodded. "Good. That way I don't have to get those worm guts all over me."

William really didn't know when the anger and frustration and hatred had begun. It just slowly took over, like a quart of black oil spreading out on the driveway from an overturned can. But it had happened, that's for sure. And it was intense. It was severe. And it was spreading.

• • •

The butterfly enjoys the sun
Enjoys the wind and breeze
Blithe.
And then the shadow of the eagle

Patty heard the knock at the door. Her jaw dropped when she opened it. That smile. Those blue eyes. The quick shiver that ran down her spine.

"Hi, honey," Roy said. He raised his hands up to the side of his face — palms forward — and shook them. "Surprise!" And then his laugh. "Look, I don't have a whole lot of time, so grab some of your things and let's go."

Patty held up her hand in shock, trying to come to terms with what was happening.

Roy slapped her hand. "Put the hand down. Let's go. We can talk in the truck."

"Roy, I can't just..."

The smile left his face immediately. And he looked hard, bitter, angry and—even evil. His look changed instantly. Patty couldn't finish the sentence.

Roy looked down at the small table next to the door. He picked up Patty's purse and handed it to her. She took it and he put his hand on the back of her neck, squeezing harder than he should. He leaned in close and whispered. "Sure is good to see you." Then he kissed her on the lips. He smiled at her again, and then he pulled her out the door. "Now let's get going."

Maggie Lancaster looked out of the car window at the pretty countryside. She was happy to be heading down the interstate toward her sister's cabin on the lake. She knew husband William needed some time off, some peace and quiet, but you know, she was looking forward to some herself. And maybe he would start talking to her again. He had been so quiet lately.

"I sure wish you'd talk to me once in a while. You know, if it wasn't for me, we wouldn't talk to each other at all, and you just keep getting worse and worse. Where it used to be an occasional sentence or two, now it's only a 'yes' or a 'no,' unless it's just a grunt here and there. Sometimes I think I'm talking to a brick wall. No communication whatsoever."

William grunted like an ape and then gave her a little smile. "Oh, William," she said, giggling, as she slapped his arm. "Always joking around." She turned on the radio and picked up a station playing a country song: "I Sure Miss My Dog Holler." She rocked back and forth in the seat for a minute, humming along, and then she turned the volume down a pinch.

"Did you remember to pack the rafts? I'm not going swimming without a raft," she said. "Remember that blue one? It had a hole in it. You didn't bring that one, did you?" William grunted again. "The yellow one is the only good one. That's the one I want." She went back to rocking in her seat. "You know, William, it's always so nice to get away and relax, and you might even talk to me, since there won't be any guys to talk to, and my sister's cabin still doesn't have any TV— so no sports—except the radio—if we can pick up the right station. Of course, if the fish are biting, I might not see you all day long. Oh, well, I'll just lie on my raft or one of those inner tubes. You know, William, an inner tube wouldn't be too bad, that is, if you didn't pack the yellow raft—even so, a change is good now and again, to keep the old monotony down, right? It sure is nice of my sister to let us use the cabin. I'm so excited and it's going to be so much fun—just the two of us—a nice, relaxing week. A little R and R is going to be nice, isn't it? I sure could use a little peace and quiet, couldn't you, William?"

Maggie went back to looking out the window. "It sure is pretty here, isn't it, William?"

FIVE

The butterfly circles
Returning again and again
To the draw of the light
Too much heat
But too much draw
Again and Again — to the light

And just like that, Patty found herself sitting once again in Roy's vehicle—a truck this time with Schrader Farms painted on the side of it. All the work she had been doing to get beyond him—undo all of his crap—and in an instant, right back into it. *I am pathetic,* she thought.

"It seems like it was only yesterday, doesn't it, Patty?" Roy said. "You are looking good. Kind of missed you lately, though. Where you been?"

"Just working and going to school, Roy. It had nothing to do with you, but all those other creeps in the pen."

"Yeah, yeah. It's not like I was lonely or anything." The sarcasm thick. "As long as you haven't been messing around with anyone. You haven't, have you?"

"No, Roy," she said. "I have no other friends."

"You got me, babe," he said, slapping her thigh—hard, and then pulling her close. Patty went to him nervously. His arm was around her, and then his hand crept down and slid inside her shirt. She grabbed his hand.

"Don't stop me, Patty. I haven't felt a woman in more than two years."

She relented. Pathetic.

"Hmm. Just like I remember," he said, and he actually licked his lips.

They drove for an incredibly long time like this. She said nothing. Roy said nothing. The radio played hip-hop. Heading west.

There was an exit with a lone gas station at the end of the ramp. Roy pulled his hand away and pulled onto the ramp. At the station, Roy began pumping gas.

After a full tank, he leaned inside. "I gotta go inside. You need anything?"

"No. I'm good."

"I got to wait for this guy here to leave first." He indicated to the left and Patty looked in that direction. There was one other car at the station. The driver was finishing up. She was a little confused about why they had to wait for this guy.

The other car pulled away — finally, and Roy straightened up. "I'll be right back, babe. Start the truck and stay here." He went inside. Patty obediently turned the key, and the truck backfired and kicked to life.

Suddenly, Roy came flying out of the store. He had a wad of bills in his left hand, and a handgun in his right.

"Let's get the fuck out of here!" he said, jumping into the driver's seat and slamming the little truck into gear.

"What did you do, Roy?"

"What do you think? I made a withdrawal."

"Roy! We're going to get arrested!"

"Like I haven't done that before." He raced down the highway. "They gotta catch us first, Patty." He smiled and looked at her. "Ain't nobody going to catch me."

Don't misunderstand. There was a time when William was truly "in love" with Maggie. After all, they had survived five years of marriage, along with practically one year of dating. But that was six years and ten billion one-way conversations ago. The times they do change — along with people. Maggie used to be so fun to be around — always enthusiastic and excited about life. She always had a joke (or would just laugh at his). So bubbly and perky and cute. She sure used to be cute. She had a little pug nose, a wide smile, and that dimple appeared on her left cheek whenever she laughed real hard. He used to see if he could get her to laugh and have that dimple "wink" at him. And it usually wasn't too difficult. She had coal black hair and dark brown eyes, and when they married she was a toned (but oh so soft) one hundred and twenty pounds. Yeah - things *do* change.

But the fact remained—he had grown to detest his life and blamed his wife. He could no longer stand the sight, smell or sound of her—especially the sound. Maybe that was because it was the most predominant and the loudest and the most consistent. Frankly, she talked all the time. And it made him want to strangle her.

These were the thoughts William had as they headed down the interstate—on their way to The Lake. Maggie looked out of the car window at the pretty countryside and seemed content for a brief moment, an oh-so-very-brief moment. But it wasn't long, and she was talking at him again.

Needless to say, it was one of the longest rides to the country he ever had the misfortune to be involved in. Five hours of constant babbling will drive any decent man over the edge, let alone one who is halfway there. He had actually resorted to playing traveling games just to keep his mind off of all the inane things Maggie was going on and on about. He would time the mileage markers with his watch, and he had it down so that precisely when the second hand hit the twelve, he was passing a mileage marker and the odometer was clicking over at exactly the same time. (It took him awhile to line these all up, but after all, that *was* the point.) And the goal, of course, was to keep the speedometer at exactly sixty miles per hour so that all the gauges and the watch would continue to click at the same time. (It was a very long drive.) At one point he thought about the mole, and how good it felt to rid himself of one of life's little problems. He wondered if getting rid of things would be the great solution to all of his life's problems.

The small, dented and rusted pickup truck was parked but still bouncing on its springs, a squeak audible in the early morning sunrise.

The birds and the squirrels in the field and the woods surrounding the truck paid no attention, and the animals spent the time looking for breakfast snacks. This truck was unusual in this quiet countryside, but nothing in the early morning had made the animals fear this metal intruder. It had gone unnoticed throughout the night, aside from an occasional snore emanating from beneath the blue plastic tarp that covered the bed of the pickup. The snoring only reminded the animals of the cows mooing in the pasture on the far side of the woods. The tarp had been hastily thrown over the bed to provide relief in the case of a thunderstorm, and quickly bungee corded down to keep it from flapping in the wind. Now from below it came a slow steady moan growing in intensity and volume, then immediately stopping at the same time the squeaking did. A man's heavy breathing and the singing of the birds were the only sounds left. After a moment he could be heard moving about, and then he said, "Nothing like morning wood, is there, Patty?" He chuckled.

A second body, lighter and quieter, began to move about under the tarp. "Just get off me, Roy," Patty said. There was even more rustling about, and then the tailgate received several sharp kicks before finally slamming down with a bang onto the rear bumper. A pair of muddy combat boots, partly hidden by crumpled up blue jeans, and the hairy legs attached to them appeared from the darkness under the tarp. Next to them came another set of legs, softer and smoother, their blue jeans crumpled only onto one leg with a dirty sock, the other leg bare except for the dirty sock attached to it. A pair of female hands helped the bare leg into the jeans, and then Patty scooted and slid out from beneath the tarp and onto the edge of the tailgate. In one movement, she slid off the tailgate and onto the ground, pulled up the jeans to her waist, and threw back her head in an effort to straighten her dark blonde hair. Perhaps a good bath was in the near future? She buttoned her jeans, then leaned down and removed the dirty socks, which she then threw into the darkness under the tarp. "We need to find a laundromat, Roy," she said, and then moved off into the trees.

Roy pulled up his pants while under the tarp, and then he slid out across the tailgate onto the ground. He was even more unkempt and in need of a better bath. He spat on the ground as he scratched his crotch, and then called out toward Patty. "I think you need to climb into that wash machine yourself, Patty. Getting a little crusty, aren't you?" Roy went around the truck and untied the tarp from around the bed. He half-assed folded it up and threw it into the bed on top of their wardrobe lying loosely, and then he rolled the spare tire on top of it all to keep it from blowing out. Patty made her way back to the truck and, as she climbed in, Roy asked her, "Did you wash your hands, Patty?" He chuckled again, and she shook her head in disgust as she slammed the door behind her. Roy climbed into the driver's seat. "Damn, Patty. Why you so pissed off all the time? Shit—you got a little of my good lovin.' The sun's out. It's a beautiful day. What more do you need? We're going to have one helluva day—I can just feel it." Roy shook his head as he turned the key in the ignition. The engine did a slow grind, then slowed some more, then finally kicked to life. As it did, a loud squeal screamed from beneath the hood and billowing white smoke blew out from the exhaust pipe and blanketed the area in fog, this time scattering the birds and the squirrels. The squeal died away at the same time the smoke stopped pumping out, and after a few seconds, the wind lifted the fog from the field. The small, dented, and rusted pickup truck pulled away and headed down the dirt road.

What seemed like three years, five months and seven weeks later (approximately), William and Maggie finally arrived at The Lake. It was always called The Lake. From as far back as William could remember, it was known only as The Lake—not Quiet Lake, its proper name, but just The Lake. And everyone called it that, too, not just William and Maggie. And to make matters worse, it wasn't even much of a lake. It was more like a glorified pond, not more than thirty acres. But William and Maggie were allowed to use the cabin, which belonged to Maggie's sister Martha and her husband Larry, at least once every summer, and since no one else really lived around there, they usually had the whole place for themselves and never saw another living soul, which, fortunately, was the case this weekend. Of course, Maggie was still talking.

"Well, William, we finally made it. Boy, that sure was a long drive. How long did it take this time? Martha claims that her and Larry made it one time in three hours, but I think she was stretching it just a tad, don't you? What do you think? It seems like it always takes us forever and a day. It had to have been five hours, right? What time did we leave? It was just before noon, wasn't it? And it's four o'clock now, so that was close to five hours, right? Well, at least we're here."

William got out and opened the trunk. A multitude of suitcases and boxes winked back at him.

"How long has it been since we've been to Martha's lake house?" she continued. "Two years? Three years? We came two years ago, didn't we? I'm pretty sure we didn't come down last year, because you got ticked that you didn't get any fishing in last year. Isn't that right? That was last year, wasn't it? What do you think? Well, anyway, I'm looking forward to a nice, quiet weekend. What about you? Are you ready for a little rest and relaxation?"

He had his tackle box in his right hand. His left hand reached for the paddle. A surge of adrenaline rushed through his body when his fingers touched the paddle, when his fist gripped the handle. A little rest and relaxation is exactly what he had in mind, but he said nothing. Instead, he took the paddle and the tackle box into the house, his knuckles white from the tightness of the grip.

"I sure hope the fish are biting," Maggie said. "Remember when we came out here with Martha and Larry that one time? Boy, we were catching fish right and left. Wasn't that the time you caught that seven pounder off that big minnow you said was the king of the bucket?" She went into her laugh. William wasn't sure what was worse—her voice or her laugh. Her laugh was not even a laugh, but more of a snort and heavy breathing kind of thing. Annoying. "The king of the bucket! Why that minnow was almost big enough to fry up itself. That was one big minnow."

He went back out to the trunk, Maggie hot on his heels. How come when he wanted her around, she was never to be found, and when he wanted her to disappear, she was locked onto his heels like a new puppy from the Humane Society? He never understood that.

"Remember that big seven pounder? Of course you do. Boy, that was a big fish. That was the biggest fish you ever nailed down here at The Lake, wasn't it?"

William nodded. Yeah, the biggest fish he ever nailed, but he had his eyes set on an even bigger fish—a hundred and sixty pounder.

"Boy, that was a big fish," she said. "If I remember right, you had a hard time getting it into the live box. It kept wanting to slide through your hands, remember? And you almost dropped it back into the lake, remember that? That would have made you mad—you don't get mad too often, but when you do, look out! Boy, if that fish would have slipped back into the lake—you would have come unglued."

William remembered the last time he had come unglued. It was with the second mole. And he knew at any time soon he could become unglued again.

For a pizza joint, the place sure was dead. Roy and Patty were the only ones in the joint except for a mom and her brat. The Brat—he must have been eleven or twelve—kept complaining about the black olives on the pizza—not that Roy blamed him or anything, but the kid went on and on and Roy was getting annoyed. The Brat had on some dumb football jersey, splattered with pizza sauce, of course. His mom looked like some ding-a-ling, an overweight brunette (with streaks of gray) who'd been eating way too much pizza these days. She'd nod, then shake her head, and then nod again—totally lost and clueless. And she had bags under her eyes you could park a Chevy in. She looked like she had had no sleep in a week, and probably hadn't, not with that brat of a son. Anyway, they were the only other ones eating in the place, and Roy liked it that way.

The pizza joint had some hoity-toity Italian looking name—Amici's Pizza—but it wasn't hoity-toity at all. There were windows across the entire front of the place, but the windows were covered with so many posters and flyers and whatnots taped to them, you could barely see out. Or in. And *that's* just the way Roy liked it. Across the top of the windows there was one long shelf full of dusty trophies with a little guy playing softball on top of each one. Most of the little guys were swinging a bat, but a couple of the trophies had the little guy throwing a ball. Eat Pizza Drink Beer and Play Softball—What a Life!

There were maybe ten round tables in the place, surrounded by all these red and white vinyl chairs with chrome legs. The floor was a combination of tile and crud and old pizza sauce—hardly hoity-toity! Toward the back was a long counter and behind it were some great neon beer signs. One even had moving parts—it had two mugs that would clang together like they do when you say "Cheers!" Yep—the beer sign was the best thing in the place.

Behind the counter was this dude working the phones. Roy guessed he was the owner or something; at least he acted like he owned the place. He was slim (that was weird, being surrounded by pizza all the time), and he had a little goatee. His red "Amici's Pizza" T-shirt was hanging out over his blue jeans, and he was wearing some pork-pie hat—his shaggy brown hair sticking out from under it. A real beatnik-looking dude. (A real loser-looking dude, too...)

Roy could see the kitchen behind him through this big hole cut out in the wall. The hole was about one foot by three foot, and Roy figured they passed pizzas through it. He could tell by the looks of it that at least the kitchen was cleaner than the floor out where they sat. And he could see a couple of cooks back there. One was some pimply faced teenage punk and the other some old fat chick. She had to be fifty-years-old and at least three hundred pounds. (Surrounded by pizza all the time.) They wore those dumb white aprons and fluffy white hats and, of course, pizza sauce was all over them. The place sure went through the pizza sauce.

Then there were the drivers—the delivery guys—at least two that Roy had seen—and these guys came and went every ten minutes or so, delivering those pies to all the Couch Taters out there. Roy noticed one guy drove a killer-looking old '82 Mustang—royal blue with big old fat tires and at least six cans of wax on it. And it had chrome everywhere. (Probably pizza sauce, too)

Robbing this place would be a cinch.

. . .

It was later—not much, maybe an hour or two. William Lancaster guessed it was around six because the sun was starting its slide down the Western horizon. He was becoming less and less aware of time.

Not that it really mattered, because, after all, he was on rest and relaxation with his wife for the weekend. Time was meaningless. And he guessed life was meaningless, too. At least Maggie's was.

The little cabin was no luxury hotel. It had a small bedroom, an even smaller bathroom, and then the "great room." It was a great room because it comprised a kitchen, dining room and living room, squashed into a twelve by twelve area. At one end was a wall-to-wall bar that found more usage as a storage area. Crap littered the top, but William knew that below the surface, the bar was well stocked, which might come in handy. Other than that, at least the stove worked, the sink drained, and three of the four kitchen chairs matched. William sat at the little table in the one "unique" chair because he was feeling a little unique himself. He was tying flies—with thoughts of tying one just right to bag a really big fish. William looked over at Maggie. She was still talking at him.

"Come on, William, haven't you got that lure twisted yet? I'm all ready to go fishing."

This was when William went into a trance. He was aware she was talking, but he was no longer hearing her. It had become one great din. "I thought that's why we came out here—to get away from it all and relax. What are you going to do? Sit there the whole time tying flies? We got all those nice, big, juicy minnows, that's what they'll go for. I bet the fish are just jumping out there. What do you think? Are you ready to go yet?"

She grabbed a can of soda out of the refrigerator. William continued to twist lures. He had sort of entered another dimension. William guessed it was like an out-of-body experience. He was somebody else at the moment—no, that's not it. He just wasn't himself anymore. Maybe it was because he knew what he had to do, but he wasn't sure if *he*, William, could do it. But somebody *else* could. And indeed, William knew it *had* to be done.

"What are you going to do—sit there and twist lures all day? Come *on*—the sun will be going down and everything. Let's GO, William."

His head was going around and around and around. The orchestra was playing louder and louder—boom *boom* BOOM *BOOM*! His world was spinning—tilting—boom *boom* BOOM! Louder and *Louder* and LOUDER! When The Nag popped the tab on her soda can, it startled him, and William's world exploded, and he jerked. It made him stab himself with the fishhook. Bleeding. It made him mad. It made him furious. He watched the blood appear on his fingertip, and it trickled down, getting hung up in that wrinkle on the inside of the finger. A little pool of blood formed before it began leaking downward again. It's funny that red is the color of blood *and* of rage. And they both come from within, and from deep down.

The orchestra began another crescendo. It was the final movement of the symphony. Slowly and softly at first, then growing and growing, getting faster and faster and louder and louder. His head began spinning again. He couldn't—he wouldn't—take another moment—the music had to STOP! The orchestra—louder and louder—boom *boom*—louder and *louder* and LOUDER! He felt like his entire body was a volcano. His head was ready to explode. Brains and lava would splatter and spill down onto his shoulders—down his shirt—onto his lap—and slowly ooze and drip onto the flowered linoleum floor.

William slowly and deliberately set the lure on the table and arose from the chair. The oar was leaning up against the kitchen counter and he grabbed it.

The Nag set her soda down on the counter. "Oh, you want to take the boat out? That might be a good idea. Maybe we can catch one of those big ones if we get out into the middle of the lake a little ways. Are you ready to go? Come on, let's go fishing."

William smiled and then swung the oar with all his might toward the side of her head. It cracked loudly when it hit. The Nag fell to the floor.

She had finally stopped talking.

"Let's go swimming instead, honey," William said, as his smile widened.

SIX

Roy nodded at Patty. "This place is as good as any," he said. All she was doing was staring down at her plate — a half a slice of pepperoni staring back at her — like it was winking at her or something. She was acting nervous. She always got so damn nervous when they needed cash. And Roy didn't know why, because she sure liked it afterwards when they had some money.

"I hate this," she said. "We're going to get caught or hurt or something."

Roy just leaned back in his chair and rolled his eyes. "Hell, we ain't gonna caught. I'm way too slick for that. Just call me Slick Roy." He leaned in closer to her. "Besides, we ain't got no choice. We're down to our last fucking dollar."

She looked at him with her puppy dog eyes. "I... I can't." And then those puppy dog eyes looked back down at that damn pizza. "I can't keep this up."

Roy shook his head. Damn women — can't live with 'em, can't live without 'em. He would have just as soon got rid of her, but he needed her to watch his backside. And he needed to watch *her* backside. She did have a great backside. Nice front side, too. She was long and thin, just the way Roy liked them. And long dirty blonde hair. But it was those pretty green puppy dog eyes that always did Roy in — and she knew it.

But he also knew just what she wanted to hear. "Look — this is the last time." This made her look back at him — she'd heard it all before. "I promise." Damn those puppy dog eyes. "I promise," he said again, just to let her know how serious he was.

She went back to staring at that pepperoni. Well, never mind if she believed him or not. He had to do it—they were broke.

Roy heard the rattle of the phone being hung up. The beatnik owner dude was off the phone. Mom and The Brat were still arguing over black olives. The cooks were busy cooking. No delivery guys in sight. The time was right. It was now or never.

"Well, here goes nothing," Roy said to Patty. She just shook her head and then buried her head in her hands. "Knock that shit off, Patty. It's not like we haven't done this before." She ignored him. This pissed Roy off. He hated it when she ignored him. She should know better. They'd "talk" about it later—Roy knew how to make her listen, and how to make her shape up, too.

Roy got up, grabbing his duffel bag. The chrome legs of the chair squeaked and squawked on the floor as it slid backwards, getting hung up on all the crap on the floor. Hell—he damn near knocked it over. Needless to say, Roy didn't bother being polite like ma always said and "push your chair back in under the table." At least ma had kept the floor clean.

Before he went to the counter, he pulled Patty's head up by her chin. She was going to look at him one way or another. He motioned to the mom and her brat. "Hey—keep an eye on them over by that fucking door." When he got no reaction from her, he squeezed her chin until it hurt. "Nod if you hear me, Patty." She nodded. "That's better," Roy said. She knew she had to do her part—she had to earn her keep or else there would hell to pay.

He strolled over to the beatnik owner, his duffel bag in hand. The owner looked at Roy and smiled, kind of goofy, like he was stoned or something. "Hey, there," he said. "What else can I get you? Another pitcher?"

Roy's hand was reaching into the duffel bag as the guy spoke, and he felt the cold hard steel of the pistol. Shivers ran up and down his spine. This was always the best part. What a rush it was to grip that handle, and slowly pull the gun from the bag and point it at someone's head. With his arm totally outstretched, the gun stopped just inches from the beatnik owner's forehead. His eyes crossed as he looked into the barrel of the gun. Now he *really* looked goofy—all cross-eyed and everything. He slowly and nervously raised his hands over his head, just like in some old Western when the posse would catch up with the outlaw. ("Stick 'em up!")

"How about everything in the register?" Roy said. "And don't try to fuck with me." He had barely quit talking when he heard Patty behind him.

"Roy!"

Roy whipped around as mom and The Brat were trying to sneak out. They were out of their chairs and walking like chickens toward the door, trying their hardest to be invisible. But walking like a chicken didn't make them look invisible; it only made them look stupid.

"Hey!" Roy yelled. The chickens froze. "What do you think this is—some kind of fuckin' game? Get down on the floor. Now!"

They did—right on top of that scum and crud and pizza sauce. Roy wondered what blood and guts would look like all mixed in with that pizza sauce. He glanced over at Patty. "Keep an eye on 'em."

Now he turned back to the owner, who hadn't budged—still had the outlaw hands up. Roy moved to the kitchen door. It was a swinging door, and he kicked it open. The two cooks jumped—scared out of their wits—shaking in their boots. Roy stood in the doorway and propped the door open with his foot. Keeping the gun pointed at the owner, his eyes remained fixed on the cooks. He gave them his meanest look. "Down on the floor or I blow his fuckin' head off! Now!" They did. Roy noticed the kitchen floor was covered in crude and scum and pizza sauce, too. He threw a box in front of the door to keep it from swinging shut—so he could keep an eye on the cooks—and turned back to the owner. "Gimme the money. Hurry up!"

The owner beatnik dude punched a cash register button and the money tray slid out. Roy could see the dead presidents looking back at him—what a sight! Roy tossed him his duffel bag. "Put all those presidents in here. All of them." The owner began pulling out one wad of bills after another. "Hurry up!" Roy yelled, and he could see it was going to be a pretty good pile of cash.

The front door had one of those ringing bells that rang when it opened. That ringing bell was the next thing everyone heard—followed by Patty calling out, "Roy!" He whipped around toward it. One of the delivery guys had returned. "Hold it..." Roy started to say. Things were beginning to move too fast and get complicated and there were too many people and why doesn't he just give him the money so they could go. "Come here," Roy said to the delivery guy. "No... Stop..." He changed his mind. (I'm in control – I'm in control – I'm in control.) "Get down on the floor! Now!"

That crummy floor sure was getting plenty of business.

Roy turned back toward the owner and, as he spun, the pistol knocked over a container of Parmesan cheese, sending the stuff all over the counter. In all the excitement, the owner had stopped stuffing the money into the bag. "Come on!" Roy yelled. "Gimme my money!" Then the phone rang. "Fuck!" Roy said. "Don't answer that!" What else could happen? Everybody was watching him – waiting – it was making him nervous. (I'm in control – I'm in control – I'm in control.) It rang again. (Stop that phone! Stop that ringing! There's nobody here!) And another ring. The beatnik glanced at it. "Don't even think of answering it!"

Roy moved toward the phone behind the counter and slipped in the sauce on the floor. He didn't go down, but he gyrated and spread his arms out to keep from falling, looking like some wild Watutsi dance. This pissed him off even more, and he jerked the telephone line out of the wall, knocking the phone onto the floor. It clattered noisily. "Come on! Gimme the fucking money!" He stopped for a second to catch his breath. (One two three...) Then he pointed the gun at the beatnik's head one more time. He had finished filling the duffel bag. "Is that all of it?"

The owner nodded.

Roy grabbed the bag and whipped around the counter to leave and almost tripped over the delivery guy on the floor. "Get outta my fuckin' way!" The delivery guy started to move. "Stop! Don't move!" Now Roy pointed the gun at *his* head. "Gimme your money, too. Now!" The delivery guy dug into his pockets. "Be careful," Roy said, as if he might have a gun or something in his pocket (Way too many movies...). He pulled out a crumpled wad of bills. There was something about old dirty money Roy just loved. It was tons better than that new clean, crisp stuff. (Although he liked that kind, too.) Roy grabbed the bills and shoved them in another pocket – his.

"Come on, Roy. Let's go." Patty was getting up out of her chair and wanting to leave. She was way too nervous.

"Shut up! I can't think!" He paused, looked around, and then grabbed the phone off the floor. A piece of plastic had busted off of it. He stuffed the phone into his duffel bag. Roy and Patty wouldn't need it, but neither did the beatnik owner dude. Roy waved the gun toward the door. "Come on, Patty! Let's go!" He didn't have to tell her twice. She was at the door in a flash. The bell jangled as she opened it. Roy turned one last time and waved the gun around, pointing it at everyone one at a time. "Don't anybody try anything funny! You hear me?" He pushed Patty out the door, and the bell clanged one more time as it closed. They jumped into the truck and the engine did its slow grind, followed by the loud squeal that screamed from beneath the hood. The billowing white smoke blew out once again from the exhaust pipe and blanketed the parking lot in fog. When the fog finally cleared, they were gone and Roy was a rich man once again.

Fortunately for William, she bled little. In fact, all he could find was a little wet spot about three inches in diameter where the oar had actually connected. He guessed it was all interior damage—brain damage, or more like it, additional brain damage. Probably a pretty good bruise, though he couldn't tell because of her pretty black hair. She always did have pretty hair. And she kept it very nice. Shampooed and clean and everything, and she was always trying something new—which turned out nice every time. It made William feel kind of bad because he had really messed up her hairdo.

Because of the magic and the spontaneity of "being in the moment," William had to fetch the car. The original plan was to "do it" when they were fishing in the boat, and that way they would already be out on the lake, making it easy to dump her in the water. But now he had to drag her all the way to the car, get her into the trunk, drive down to the boat, get her in the boat, take her out into the lake, and finally dump her overboard. Oh well, a man's got to do what a man's got to do. The moment had just seemed so right at the time.

William decided to first take a walk, to clear his head a bit, and he sat by the lake. The last time he was at the lake, it had seemed so quiet and peaceful. Serene. Tranquil. Now all he heard was the croaking of those damn bullfrogs. It sounded like some crazed symphony's tuba section, all warming up at the same time—but everybody playing a different song in a different tempo in a different key. He about jumped out of his skin when one splashed into the water as he was making his way down along the shoreline. William picked up a rock to squash him, but alas, the frog had vanished. He shot-putted the rock into the water, anyway. The *kerplunk* quieted all the other tubas. But it was surely a temporary solution, for he knew they'd start up again.

He came across another rock—a smooth, flat one about the shape and size of a brick. He picked up this rock, and holding it, sat down on a log. The circles from the first *kerplunk* splash were petering out, and the little waves that were generated lapped at the shore. That was all he heard. It was deathly quiet now that the tubas had shut up. If he listened real close, he noticed how each successive lap of the water was just a little bit softer. Then again, it might just have been his overactive imagination. He wasn't sure.

A snake went swimming by. He couldn't tell what kind, although it didn't matter; it held no interest for him, and William wasn't about to go anywhere—even if it was poisonous. It kind of reminded him of himself, moving about silently to no one's attention. He shot-putted his new rock towards it and nailed the snake. It splashed about spastically, not knowing what had just happened, then nothing, disappearing, as more little ripples lapped at the shore.

A breeze kicked in. He thought he smelled a touch of Chanel No. 5 coming from her direction, but that was crazy. Stagnant old lake water was more like it. How's that for a fragrance? Stagnant Old Lake Water No. 5. He should have gone into marketing. Maybe he missed his calling.

Yeah, he was drifting. Drifting out to sea.

He lay back onto the old leaning tree so he could gaze up at the clouds slowly floating across the blueness. The tree was wet, and he felt it seeping through his T-shirt. He didn't care. It was already dirty and sweaty, and come to think of it, there was probably some blood on it. He made a mental note to double-check that later. His fingers felt a little sticky, so he got up to rinse them off in the lake. The dead snake, now upside down, floated by. He sank another rock on top of it. Maybe because it had felt good the first time, he figured it would feel good again, but it didn't. After all, it was already dead. The thrill was gone.

Such was life. Killing the Nag was satisfying, even exciting. After all, it put an end to the incessant talking and gabbing and blabbering and yakkety-yak yak yak—but he didn't feel like finishing the job, even though it had to be done: her body wouldn't go away by itself. He had to dispose of it. Somehow, he had to finish the dirty deed. William figured he should quit procrastinating and get the car. He would dump her in the trunk and that way, if she leaked, it wouldn't be so hard to clean up. He slowly made his way back to the cabin, leaving the bullfrogs playing their tubas to their own lives in the lake.

The Nag was still there and still silent (still still?). He put his hands under her armpits and started dragging her toward the door. He sure was glad she had gone on that diet at the beginning of the year. Last summer, she would have been a lot harder to maneuver when she had maxed out at one-eighty.

After a little grunting and groaning, William finally got her in the trunk of the Ford. Deadweight of that mass is not the easiest thing to move around, but he worked one side at a time, and she finally flopped in. Her arm rested on the back of the car and he had to lift it in and place it next to her. Of course, it was her left hand, and he noticed her wedding ring. ('Til death do us part.) Anyway, she was in. (Those old Fords sure had big trunks. Hell, he could've gotten two or three wives in there.)

Dusk was setting in, and it was getting dark when he slammed the trunk lid. And then he saw the headlights coming through the trees.

•   •   •

Patty once again hated her life. It was one big ugly cycle, spinning from one bad thing to another, only to do it all over again in a day, maybe even a week. It all depended on how much money Roy "made." But no matter how much he made, it always ran out, and they would have to do it again. Oh, he'd be as happy as a lark for a while, and drunk for longer than that. When he was "up," things were fine, but then he'd drink too much and crash and be ugly and mean and… everything else.

"We got some bucks now, Patty." Roy was all smiles at the moment. He was driving their little truck, and he'd slap the wheel each time he came up with something "cute" to say. "Give me a slice of pizza with extra cheese, sir! Ha Ha!" Once upon a time these used to be cute, but she just didn't see the cuteness in them anymore. If she could only run away from him... but she couldn't even think about it. He'd know somehow what she was considering, and that would just throw him into a rage. But if she did leave, maybe she'd be happier. But no—he'd only hunt her down. She knew that.

Roy immediately sensed Patty's mood. That was one of his few talents (or one of Patty's curses). "Cheer up, honey. All we gotta do is find a place to crash for a couple of days. Lie low for a while and everything will be cool again." He snapped his fingers. "Do you know we cleared almost six hundred bucks on that last deal? Six hundred bucks! We're rich!" Roy crumpled up the can of his first beer. Of course, they had made the liquor store their first stop "after work." The truck had one of those rear windows that slid open. He tossed the empty can into the back of the truck through the open window. "Grab a couple of more beers, honey." He looked at her empty hands. "Hell, you ain't even started yet. Come on! What are you waiting for? Let's celebrate!" Patty didn't feel much like celebrating. "Come on!" he said, but still she didn't move. Something was holding her back.

Roy grabbed her arm, squeezing too hard—way too hard. It hurt. "Get me a fucking beer! If you don't want one, that's your problem. But you're gonna get me one now!"

The cold beers were in the bed of the truck as well. A large cooler within reach from inside—with the ice mostly turned to water. Patty slowly turned and half-leaned, half-climbed through the back window. She looked past the truck bed and behind the truck. The two-lane country highway was disappearing behind them. Each new hill they went over hid them from where they had come. She wasn't sure if that was good or bad. She wasn't sure of anything.

Roy slapped her butt. From his angle, it was an easy target. "Ah— your good side. You're looking better every day, Patty." He laughed and slapped her butt again, this time even harder. Patty didn't think any of this was "cute" either. "Hurry up. I'm thirsty."

She quickly grabbed a couple of beers and climbed back into the cab, handing one to Roy.

"Open it up. It's hard enough to drive these old highways without having to fiddle with a beer." He swerved to "make his point," and almost hit a car head on. Patty gasped, and he laughed. "It's good to see I can still make you squirm."

She popped the top of the beer and gave it to him. He slurped down a sizeable portion of it in one swallow. She popped the other one and took a sip. It tasted horrible for some reason, so she set it in the little plastic can holder that hung under the window on top of the door—one of their 99-cent upgrades. It had been blowing in the wind until she set the can in there. That quieted it down. She was somewhat quieted down, too. She just stared blankly out the window and watched as they passed one country house after another.

Roy shook his head. Whenever he was in a good mood, he just figured the entire world was happy. "Sometimes you act awful weird, Patty. If I didn't know any better, I'd think you wasn't happy."

"I'm just quiet today, that's all," she lied.

They traveled for a good hour or two—passing through maybe a half a dozen small country towns—and more than a few beers. She never knew what kind of place Roy would pick for them to stay. Well, she knew it would not be something nice, but she didn't know if they would have a roof over their heads or sleep under the stars—like last night—under the blue tarp. They usually slept under the stars when they were low on cash, so Patty was hoping for a bed since they "were rich." It had been six nights since she had last slept in a bed—other than the bed of the truck, that is. And a shower would be nice, too. Especially for Roy, if he'd even bother. But other than the smell, he wore it well. He always looked pretty good. He had a good complexion, considering how little he used soap. And his gray-blue eyes were so pretty. He reminded a lot of people of a young Paul Newman, and he played it to the hilt. He'd wink at little old ladies every chance he got, and they'd giggle like schoolgirls. Funny how Roy got his kicks, although Patty had to admit he had that same effect on her, which is one reason she was still around. Of course, the other reason was stupidity on her part. She just wished he'd only be a little nicer.

"Another brewskee, please," he said, wiping his mouth with the back of his hand. She hadn't even touched hers since putting it in the plastic can holder. He was really "slamming 'em." Patty silently prayed the sun would go down soon, because maybe he'd pull over for the night. Needless to say, she didn't like his driving after six or seven beers, but there was nothing she could do or say to stop him—or slow him. In fact, she knew if she made any kind of negative comment, it would only egg him on to keep going—and faster.

So she got him another beer. He had bought an eighteen-pack, so there was no hope of running out. They had gotten a little warmer though—all the ice now melted—so maybe she could convince him to stop for more ice. Once he stopped, it was hard to get him going again. He always found someone to gab with. He could go on with total strangers forever.

The sun was moving down the sky. It'd set within the hour. That was good.

"I gotta pull over to take a piss, Patty. Keep an eye out for a good spot."

Patty looked ahead and saw a gravel road coming up fast on the right. Roy saw it, too, and slowed quickly. The truck pulled a little to the left, and he jerked the wheel to the right to correct it. "I gotta look at those brakes," he said as he took the turn onto the gravel road too fast and the truck slid and skidded. The rear-end fishtailed into the tall grass that lined the road. Patty held her breath to keep the gasp from escaping. Roy somehow managed to straighten the truck, and they barreled down the gravel road. He chuckled. "That was close, wasn't it?" Patty exhaled slowly. They were leaving a monstrous dust cloud behind the little truck, and she could hear the occasional rock hitting the inside of the wheel well. As they sped along, she gripped the handle of the door with all her might, and Patty pressed her feet hard to the floorboard.

The gravel road gave way to a dirt road, but nothing much changed except they lost the cloud of dust behind them. That must have made a difference to Roy, because he suddenly slammed on the brakes. The brakes locked, but they just slid in the grass and dirt, finally coming to rest after a ten-yard slide. In one motion, Roy opened the door, jumped out and was going to the bathroom. She had to listen to him going, and she had to hear him say "Ahh..." She didn't know how many times she had had to listen to him do this. Once is enough, of course, but it didn't matter what Patty thought.

He finished and was back in the truck. "Now I got room for a few more," he said with a smile. The truck pulled away. Roy was looking around and squinting through the trees. "I wonder what's down this way." He looked over at her. "It's got to go somewhere, right?"

They ambled down the road. "Hey, look at that, Patty." He pointed through the trees on the right side of the truck. She turned and saw the sunset reflecting off the surface of a lake. "Feel like swimming, darlin'?" They kept on going. "And there's a little cabin. Looks like we'll be sleeping inside tonight."

Patty let out a big sigh. This night might not be too bad after all. But then she saw a car parked by the cabin, and she feared they might not be alone. That would not be good.

"We're home, mom!" Roy said loudly and laughed. The truck moved down the road toward the car. Then Patty saw a man stand up from behind the car as he slammed down the trunk lid. Her heart rate quickened once again.

PART THREE

ONE

William could see the little dusty truck approaching through the trees, but he could not believe it. He would have bet there had not been another vehicle on the dirt road to the cabin between the time Larry's had pulled out and his had pulled in yesterday. Why now? Somebody must be lost. Or a needy neighbor looking for a cup of sugar. Most likely a nosy neighbor wondering who could be staying at Larry's place, as if they needed to care.

William moved around to the front of the car. No reason for him to hang out with Maggie at the rear of the car. She was presently quiet, but if anyone could talk after death, it would be Maggie. William listened to the tires crunching through the gravel and dirt as the truck pulled to a stop in front of him. He could see now it was red and old, not just dusty and old. Between the evening dusk and the headlights shining in his face, William could not see details too well, but he could make out that there were two people in the cab. Just great. The more NOT the merrier.

The engine was turned off, and both doors opened and shut. The passengers met in front of their truck, and with the headlights still on, they were in silhouette for William — nothing but black shadows.

"Hello there," the driver said. It was a man's voice. It sounded young, but William wasn't sure. William saw longish hair on the passenger — so it was either a woman or a hippie. He couldn't tell yet.

"Can I help you? You lost?" William didn't want to sound too nice — too inviting. He wanted to sound like he hoped they would *get* lost.

"Well, yes, to both questions." They moved in a little closer to him and he caught a strong whiff of beer. "We was trying to find the Silver Saddle Campground. No luck."

William paused and cocked his head. He tried to sound as disinterested as possible. "I can't help you. I'm not from around here."

"Gee, that's too bad." The man paused. He definitely had an air of confidence about him. He pointed back toward the truck. "We got all our gear and stuff—just nowhere to set up camp."

He waited. William waited. William figured he knew where this was headed, and he didn't like it. He wasn't about to give them any ideas about an open invitation to stay.

"How about letting us set up camp in the field right there?" There it was. The man pointed with his thumb over his left shoulder. He didn't turn around and look in that direction. Just pointed like he had already staked it out and knew the exact spot where they would go. "Hell, you wouldn't even know we was here. We'd be gone in the morning."

This was not supposed to happen. William shook his head and spread his hands, palms up, in front of him. "Look, I'm expecting people tomorrow." He couldn't help but steal a look in the direction of Maggie. He wasn't lying. If they didn't get out of there, he'd be expecting Maggie to (still) be there in the morning. "I'd really like to help you, but..." William left the statement drag without closure.

"Hey, I said we'd be gone," the man shot back quickly. "We'll clean up any mess we make. Look, it'd be even cleaner than it is now."

William just stayed silent. Didn't the man get it? Get lost.

"Me and my girl, that's Patty there—we're beat."

William looked in her direction. So it was a girl. That was somewhat comforting. Although William guessed, for all he knew, she could be as mean as a wildcat. William turned back to the man. "Look, buddy. I'm tired, too." He glanced back at their truck. (Subliminal message to the guy: Get in this truck and LEAVE. It didn't work. The guy didn't budge. He was determined to screw up William's night.) "I came all the way out here to relax," William said. "My wife will be here tomorrow—with her sister—and I plan on fishing all night. You understand, right? Boys' night out. That kind of thing."

"Yeah, I understand," he shot back. "I also understand that we won't bug ya. You won't even know we're here."

The girl spoke. "Come on, Roy. Let's go."

"I ain't going nowhere." William could hear the agitation in the man's voice. William could see the next step in this conversation—not good. Roy took a deep breath and turned to the girl. "Look, Patty, I want to treat you right."

"Let's just leave this nice man alone. We'll find a place." That was more like it, William thought. The girl had the right idea.

Unfortunately, the guy would have no part of it. "Mister, can we stay here—*please*?" The sarcasm in his voice was thick. "We won't be a bother—honest."

William held his ground. Maybe the girl could talk some sense into her boyfriend. "I'd like to help, but…"

What he did next, William couldn't believe. The man actually reached behind his back and pulled out a pistol that had been tucked into his pants. William had never had a gun pointed at his head, and he had to admit it was rather uncomfortable. When Roy actually pulled back the hammer, William really got nervous.

"Let's move toward that fuckin' cabin, mister." He motioned toward the cabin with the gun. It glistened in the twilight. William did not appreciate Roy waving that thing around—loaded and ready to fire.

"Roy, don't do this," the girl pleaded.

He exploded. "Shut up!" With his free hand, he grabbed her by the collar and brought her face close to his. "We got a nice place to stay now." With his hand to her forehead, he shoved her backwards, and she almost fell to the ground. "Get my bag, Patty." She hesitated for a second, and he turned and glared at her. "Move!" She did.

Roy turned his attention back to William. William's attention remained on the loaded weapon as Roy waved it again. "Let's go, mister." William slowly turned away from him and headed toward the cabin. He really didn't want to turn his back on the pistol, but it seemed he had no other choice.

Inside, Roy continued to wave the pistol around, gesturing to William to sit down at the table. Patty dropped their bag and stood across from him, at which time Roy went snooping around the bar, of course.

In the light, they looked more run-down than William had imagined. Both wore blue jeans ripped up and covered in holes. Both of their pants were covered with dirt and grime. He had on a flannel shirt with the sleeves ripped off. A big tattoo of an American flag was on his left bicep. She wore a white T-shirt under a grey windbreaker.

"Lookie here," Roy said as he pulled a bottle of whiskey from behind the bar. He grabbed a glass and poured it full. As he raised it, he looked at William and said, "Cheers," then he drained the glass and slammed it down on the bar. "Not bad," he said, as he wiped the back of his hand across his mouth. Then he lit a cigarette and slowly blew out the smoke. "Pour me another one, bartender." He looked around sheepishly. "Oh, that's me." And then he laughed a loud, obnoxious laugh. He grabbed the bottle again and drained the rest of it into the glass, and then he slammed the empty bottle into the trashcan. It landed hard on something and it shattered into pieces. This amused him, so he chuckled. The gun began to hang lazily in his grip, and William was glad to see he had put the hammer back in the safe position (as if a pistol had a "safe" position). Roy thought he was a real tough guy, and he was drunk and scary—and well-armed—but every time he did something, William couldn't help thinking this guy was an imbecile. Maybe that made him even more dangerous.

Patty's eyes darted about the room. She spotted the hallway beyond the bar. "Mister, is there a bathroom back there?"

William looked toward Patty. "Yes, there is. Help yourself."

Roy butted in. "Damn straight, she'll help herself. We'll do any fuckin' thing we want."

Patty opened their little bag and dug around for a bit, finally pulling out a toothbrush and toothpaste. She dug around a little more, and then figured that was all she needed out of there. She took off her jacket and moved down the hallway. Roy stopped her as she passed. "I bet there's even running water in this place. What do you think of that? Five star, huh?" He slapped her backside as she went by him, harder than he really should have, as usual, and she scooted off to the bathroom quickly.

"Yeah, he kept calling me 'dude.' And then when he left, it was in this old truck—a small one—and, man, did it backfire. Holy hell—sounded like a 44 magnum."

Officer Downey folded his arms. "You sure, Homer? You ever heard a 44 magnum? Those suckers will melt your eardrums."

"Put a hole in you the size of a coffee can, too," Officer Blakey added.

"No kidding." Officer Downey nodded. "I went deer hunting with one a couple of years ago. Remember? Blew a hole in that buck I shot. I could've stuck my whole hand in there. Damn near half my arm, probably."

"I remember that. That was a pretty excellent shot, too."

"Thank you."

"Guys," Homer said. He owned Amico's Pizza and was trying to get the robbery into the police books. "Mind getting back on topic?"

"I thought we were talking about 44 magnums."

"No, man. We were talking about the truck backfiring."

"Oh, yeah. What color was it, dude?" The two officers laughed at Officer Downey's 'dude' reference. "Did you get the license plate number? Dude?"

"No—there was a lot of smoke when it started. By the time the smoke cleared, they were long gone."

"Well, that's not a lot of help, Homer."

"Shit, I know. I was just glad he didn't shoot me, you know? You know what it's like to have a pointed at you?"

"Homer, we're professionals," Officer Blakey said. "'Gun-pointed-at-me' is my middle name."

"Remember that time that one bozo pointed a shotgun at you? You want to shake in your boots, dude, have someone point a shotgun at you."

"No kidding. Ain't no missing with a shotgun."

"Blood and guts would go everywhere. Look like pizza topping all over the place, you know, Homer?"

"That's not nice."

"By the way—you got any extra pies lying around?"

"No kidding. I'm starving."

"I got a pepperoni that someone ordered and never picked up. It was old Mr. Olson. He does that all the time: orders a pie and then forgets he did. It's been warming for an hour." Homer retrieved the large pizza, and they all dug in. "Now, can we get back to business, please? Robbery is not the least bit funny."

"Oh yeah, yeah, yeah," Officer Downey agreed, licking sauce off of his thumb. "Any distinguishing marks? Anything weird about either of them?"

"No, not really." Homer thought for a second. "The girl had a nice butt on her."

Officer Downey chuckled, and Officer Blakey shook his head. "That'll help. Did you get that, Officer Downey?"

"Yep—nice butt. So anyone we pull over, we'll say, 'Please get out of the car, and turn around, please.'"

Now Officer Blakey chuckled. "No kidding."

"Nope—this one is not our girl. You'd be Big Ass Bertha."

They both laughed.

"Not our girl." They laughed again. "Homer, we were thinking maybe a scar, or a mole, or something like that. Maybe one of them limped? Missing a finger?"

"No—nothing like that. Oh yeah, a tat of an American flag on his arm. Left one."

"There you go. That'll help." Officer Downey picked up another slice of pizza. "Good pie, Homer."

"Thanks."

"We'll check around and see if anyone else knows anything about a backfiring little truck, but I imagine they are long gone by now."

"Yep—probably in the next state—or further—robbing some other poor sap." Officer Blakey glanced at Homer. "Not that you're a sap or anything, dude."

The two officers laughed again and then ate more pizza.

Patty shut the bathroom door and for a moment leaned with her back to it, rested, and took in the little room. It wasn't much, but it did have running water, along with a toilet, and something she hadn't seen for a while: a shower. She took a deep breath and found herself almost smiling. When she opened the closet door to see what was inside, the smile spread across her face. There inside was a wash machine. Patty couldn't remember the last time she had clean clothes. She rushed back to Roy, who was still planted at the bar, finishing off yet another drink.

"Roy, they have a wash machine," she said excitedly. "Do you want me to wash your clothes?"

Roy set his glass down. "What are you saying? You think I stink?"

She shook my head quickly. "No, of course not, Roy. But wouldn't it be nice to have clean clothes?"

He now shook his head and turned back to his drink. "I don't need no fuckin' clean clothes. Knock yourself out though." He glanced at the man. "You got anything she can change into around here?"

The man at the table looked from Roy to Patty. "In the bedroom back there is a dresser that has some odds and ends. I'm not sure what all is in there, but you should be able to find something."

Roy looked back at her. "There you go. Five star accommodations."

Patty turned and went back down the hallway to the other room on the right—the bedroom. This was another small room and in it was a double bed and a dresser with a lamp sitting on it. That was it, and that was about all there was room for. She turned on the lamp and opened the top drawer. In it were assorted towels on the left and clean bed sheets on the right. She grabbed one towel and opened the bottom drawer, this one filled with various T-shirts, shorts and swimming suits, both men's and women's. She looked through the T-shirts and found one with a motorcycle on it—too large for her, but she didn't care. From the pile of shorts she found some blue jean cut-offs that might not be too big, so she grabbed those and headed back to the bathroom.

Patty closed the door again and took another deep breath. She didn't like that they forced themselves into the place, but she had to admit that the shower and wash machine looked super good, and she was glad they were there. If only Roy would quit drinking so much. It changed him and made him so mean. He'd get himself so worked up and mad, and then he usually took out his frustration on her in some form or another—some physical form or another. Patty set the towel and fresh clothes on the sink and removed what she had on. She wanted to get her old, dirty clothes laundered as fast as she could, so she dropped them into the wash machine and hit "normal load." The beautiful water began filling the machine.

When she turned around, she caught her reflection in the mirror and it made her pause. The bruise on her right shoulder was not as dark as it had been the last time she looked, but she could still see it, and the blueness made her angry. Roy could be such a pig when he was drinking. Maybe because there was a third person around, she would be safe for once. He was careful not to hurt her breasts, of course, so they looked just the way he liked them. And the little butterfly tattoo he insisted she get—just above her tan line and a couple of inches below her belly button—looked sadly back at her, as if it was wishing it could fly free. Patty twisted around and studied her back. It was clear and free from any bruises, although there were two sets of four scratch marks thanks to Roy's longish fingernails. And her butt was red from where Roy had just slapped it. She turned the water on and searched in the closet for shampoo and soap, and found these along with a washcloth. When Patty stepped into the water, the warmth was so soothing. She just stood there, her back to the cascading water, with her forehead leaning on the shower wall, and she let the water pour over her sore and aching body, and she watched the water at her feet turn a shade of brown. This brown water swirled and went down the drain—drain away, drain away. After the warm water slowly became clear again, Patty straightened and soaped up the washcloth. Her plan was to stay in there until all the hot water ran empty, so she moved slowly and methodically as she cleaned herself. She wasn't sure when she might have this luxury again.

When Patty washed her face, she felt the tenderness in both cheeks. Roy was an equal opportunity employer when it came to hitting her cheeks—and he was equally good with both fists. Fortunately, it had been several days since he had last punched her and the mark on her left cheek had all but disappeared, although still sore to the touch. Her right cheek hardly hurt at all anymore. Roy could be so brutal at times, but then oh so tender at others—and always begging forgiveness and "making up" afterward. Patty thought it was the "making up" that he enjoyed the most, and she had to admit these were her favorite times, too. Not really much of a choice. He actually made love instead of just fucking—but yeah, she knew he enjoyed fucking at times, too.

Patty found a razor in the soap dish, and she made use of this great luxury. Wow—clean and smooth skin. She almost felt like a woman again. As she finished, she felt the water turn a shade cooler, so she turned that beautiful water off and stood there a moment and watched the remaining droplets run down her body. She even scooped a couple up in her fingertips and brought them to her lips. Water—life blood.

She stepped out of the shower and gazed at her reflection again. Yes, there's the Patty she remembered. She smiled at herself briefly, then slowly the smile faded. Patty put on the blue jean shorts and found they fit her rather nicely. The T-shirt was huge, but with no bra on, it was probably just as well.

Her eyes went to the small glass shelf to the right of the mirror. On it she found a small collection of make-up. Patty picked up the base and opened it slowly. She'd almost forgotten how to apply the stuff, but she liked how it covered the remains of the bruise on her left cheek. She darkened her lashes with mascara and blinked at herself like a cover girl. This produced another smile and the evidence of pale lips. She picked up the two shades of lipstick—neither one a color she would ever purchase—but opted for the lighter red none-the-less.

Patty stepped back to take in her entire reflection. Who was this gorgeous young woman staring back at her? Who was the young girl that first stepped into the bathroom? Were they even the same person? Patty definitely liked the one standing before her; the other one she was not so sure about.

The buzzing of the wash machine jolted her from her thoughts and back to reality. She heard Roy yell from the other room.

"What the hell are you doing back there for so long, Patty?"

She pulled her clothes from the wash machine and brought them to her face. She inhaled long and deep and relished their smell — or rather lack-there-of. Spring fresh — wow.

"Get your ass out here, Patty. I wanna play poker."

She took one last deep breath and then hung her clothes over the top of the shower door to dry. Alas, no dryer. Then she sighed and left the bathroom — back to Roy.

TWO

Back at the bar, Roy set the pistol down and spotted the man's tackle box sitting at the far end of the bar. "It says 'William' here. That you?"

William just stared at him.

Roy didn't like this. "I said—is that you?"

William finally nodded.

"What the fuck do you do for fun around here?" Roy looked around and then nodded. "Oh yeah. Go fishing." He shook his head and opened the deck of playing cards he had found at the end of the bar. "You play cards, William? Or is it Willy Boy?" He chuckled again. With the deck of cards, he sauntered over to the table (all the time waving the pistol, of course). Then he fetched his fresh drink (and the second bottle of whiskey), before returning to William at the table, sitting/falling down hard in the chair next to him.

Roy held the gun to William's head and said, "We're gonna play cards." Like he was the real Jesse James or something. "We'll wait for Patty, though. Poker is always better with three people." He slammed the next drink, then picked up the fresh bottle and read the label, like he was some kind of whiskey connoisseur or something. "This is pretty good stuff. You got good booze, and all this..." He raised his arms (still with the pistol, of course) and looked around quickly. "You must be really rich or something."

William said nothing and looked at Patty as she entered from behind Roy. Wow—he had to admit she cleaned up nicely. And he had never seen those shorts look so good—especially never on his sister-in-law, that was for sure.

As Patty sat down at the table, Roy looked at her. He cocked his head to the left and then smirked. "What the hell we have here? You all gussied up and everything. Where the fuck do you think you're going? To the prom or something?" He reached out and wiped her left cheek with his thumb. She leaned back, and he opened his hand as if to slap her, but then stopped. "You covered up your love-marks and everything." He leaned back and took her all in one more time. "Not too bad, I guess. Shit, I just might have to fuck you later." He smiled. "And maybe slap all that make-up shit off of you. What do you think about that, Patty?"

William looked at Patty, and he could tell she was extremely nervous—more like terrified. Roy set the gun down on the table, pointing in the direction of William, and still within easy reach. He opened the deck of cards and started to shuffle. "I take it you know how to play poker. It's me and Patty's favorite game. Although we usually play a variation of the game that makes it a lot more fun—if you know what I mean." He smiled broadly, then glanced at Patty and softly stroked her hair. He looked back, pointing a finger at William. "We ain't playing that version tonight though, Willy Boy."

William shot another glance at Patty. She wasn't laughing. She was looking down at her fingers crossed in front of her on the table. When she had come out of the bathroom, her hair had been swept back. Now it was covering much of her face. It was light brown—straight and cut short above the shoulders. She looked like a tomboy, but William figured she would be rather striking cleaned up like this in a prom dress. At the moment, she just looked scared and nervous.

Roy began dealing out a round of five-card draw to the three of them. "I'll ask you again: do you know how to play poker, Willy?"

William just stared at Roy and said nothing.

Roy stopped dealing and glared at him. "You know, I really hate it when someone ignores me." He took a sip (surprise surprise) and finished dealing the cards. "Good thing I got a soft heart, Willy Boy. I'll let it slide this time."

William continued to stare back at Roy. Patty repeatedly looked from her hands to Roy to William. Roy looked at his cards and then looked at William. "Look at your cards and tell me how many you want."

William picked up his cards and looked at them. He looked back at Roy. "Two."

Then Roy looked toward Patty. "How many do you want, honey?" It was then he noticed that Patty's cards were still on the table. "Pick up the damn cards and tell me how many you want. Now!"

Patty picked up the cards and absent-mindedly looked at them. She whispered "Two."

Roy cocked his head, and he leaned toward her. "What? I didn't hear you."

"Two."

Roy dealt the two cards to Patty, then he picked up his hand. He set down one card and dealt himself a fresh one. Roy picked up his new hand, smiled, and looked at William. "Whaddya got, Willy Boy?"

William had never stopped staring at Roy, and he kept his eyes on Roy as he threw down his hand. "A pair of tens."

Roy's smile grew larger. He turned to Patty. "What about you?"

Patty threw her hand down on the table to reveal a pair of sevens.

Roy smiled broadly and laughed. "I got three fours. I win." He gathered the cards and pushed the deck toward William. "You ain't much of a poker player, are you, Willy Boy?"

William shook his head and looked from Roy to Patty. He began shuffling the cards. Patty returned to looking down at her hands. Roy returned to drinking and then set his empty glass down on the table.

After he finished shuffling, William thought he might stir the pot a little. "Are you enjoying your stay, Patty?"

Roy stopped short. "Hey, mister. Quit flirting with my girl."

"Roy, calm down," she said. "And quit drinking so much."

"Hell, you gotta drink whiskey if you play poker." He looked at William with his bloodshot eyes. "Ain't that right, poker face?" And then the loud laugh again.

"I'm sorry, mister," she said. "He gets like this every once in a while. He doesn't mean anything by it."

For a guy as drunk as he was, Roy still had quick reflexes. His fist whipped out in a backhand at Patty—connecting with her jaw. William heard the blow before he saw it. Out of instinct, William jumped up, his chair falling over behind him. He tackled Roy, and the two crashed to the floor. The pistol flew to the floor and skidded a few feet away.

William got the first punch in, but he really wasn't much of a fighter, and Roy maneuvered himself on top of William and commenced to punch him again and again. But William put up a good fight, covering his face, and flopping around enough to knock Roy away. Roy went to jump up, but William grabbed his foot and he tumbled back to the floor. Roy landed a kick to William's head. William was bleeding pretty good now—from his nose and mouth—and the kick dazed him. Roy jumped up, ready to kick him some more.

"Stop it, Roy!" It was Patty. Roy glanced at her. She held the gun and pointed it at Roy.

"Really, Patty." Huffing and puffing. "You're gonna shoot me?" He kicked William again, and William grunted and moaned.

"Stop, Roy!" She sniffled, and her jaw had become red and puffy.

"I'll tell you what," Roy said, grabbing some rope from the side of the bar. "You shoot me now, so when I'm done tying up, Willy Boy, I don't kick your ass. How's that sound?"

The gun began to quiver.

"While you decide, Patty, I'm going to get busy." Roy flipped William onto his stomach. Drops of blood flew from his nose and landed on the floor. "You're a mess, Willy Boy." He pulled William's hands behind him and tied them tight. Patty's entire arms began to shake, and she was having a hard time keeping the gun raised. Her neck stiffened and her teeth clenched together.

"Please don't accidentally pull the trigger, Patty," Roy said. "All that shaking you're doin' is makin' me nervous." Then Roy looped the rope around his legs and tied his ankles tight, too. "Hog-tied. Yee hah!"

William rolled over and moaned one more time. Patty's eyes began to roll back in her head, and she was having difficulty breathing. Her body shaking now—the gun in her hands moving back and forth—up and down. When her head started shaking, she had to turn away.

"What's wrong, Patty? Don't like seeing someone tied up?" Roy went to her and easily took the gun. She was trying to regain her composure—regain smooth breathing and a steady heartbeat. "You know what I don't like?" He grabbed her chin and tugged it to face him. Her eyes were glazed. "I'll tell you what I don't like. Someone pointing a gun at me. Especially my girl." He punched her hard in the stomach and she doubled over. Then he grabbed her and threw her to the floor. Roy turned her onto her back, and sat down hard on her hurt stomach, straddling her like a pony. He slapped her with his left hand. And then slapped her with his right. Roy picked up another piece of rope and let it swing in front of Patty's face.

"Lookie what we have here, Patty?"

She began to shake violently now. Roy had a harder time holding her down, but it only seemed to amuse him all the more. He laughed. She was rocking back and forth, shaking up and down, and strange sounds were coming from her throat. Her eyes were completely rolled back. She was flopping around so hysterically that Roy couldn't hog-tie her like he wanted to, but opted for tying her hands in front of her, and then tying her feet separately.

"Damn, Patty—you're making me work way too hard," he said, wiping the sweat off of his brow. He sat back and admired his handiwork. William wasn't moving, but he was watching—disgusted. Patty was having some sort of a seizure. But being tied up, her movements were kept to a minimum. Roy watched, intrigued by her actions. The seizures became less and less, and slowed down to the point she was only quivering again—her whole body, of course, but only slight shakes now. Roy leaned back and shut his eyes for a second. That was enough. He passed out.

⋅ ⋅ ⋅

Patty was sore. She couldn't move. Slowly, things came back into focus. She saw the knots on her hands. Felt the knots on her ankles. The hyperventilating began. She closed her eyes. She forced herself to refocus. *Can I beat this?* The tremors returned. *Can I beat this?* Focus. Focus. *I can beat this.*

She slowly opened her eyes again. The knots were still there on her wrists. Of course. But she could reach one of them with her right hand. Focus on the knot. Not on being tied. Focus on untying the knot. Don't think about being tied up.

Her index finger could touch it. Pull on it. It moved. Focus. Pull. Focus. The knot loosened. A little at a time. *I'm tied up!* Breath slow. *I can't move!* Her body shook. Her eyes rolled back in her head. The lights flashed. She couldn't breathe. She was fading again. It was growing dark. *What was I doing? What should I do?* Untie the knot. Focus on the knot. The knot can be beat. The knot is not the enemy. Focus. Untie. One end came loose. The knot released. She pulled it apart. She yanked it off of her wrists. Slow the breathing. Relax. Focus. *My hands are free.* Patty leaned her head back and took a deep breath. Clearing. *Clear my head.* Focus. *I'm not done. Untie my feet.* Looking down. *I'm tied up. I can't move.* Focus. Focus. Grab the knot. Loosen. Loosen! *I can do this. I can do this.* The knot is loose. The knot is free. *My legs are free. I am free!*

Patty stood up and caught her breath. Staring at the rope at her feet. She kicked it across the floor in disgust. *Get away from me.* Patty slowly looked around and then realized: *I am free.*

Roy was lying on the floor. Passed out. The pig.

William, too, on the floor. Snoring. Dried blood on his face. Some on the floor.

Her jaw was sore. Her stomach hurt. She walked to the freezer and quietly put some ice into a washrag. It felt good on her jaw. She walked back to the bathroom and looked in the mirror—the last time so happy with who looked back at her. This time—only shame.

Her jaw was red, but not too swollen. And none of her teeth seemed loosened. Patty wiped her eyes where the mascara had run. He had done it to her again. *You know, it's kind of funny. He'll be as nice as can be when he wakes up.* She told herself that was his greatest lie. He was not a nice person. She had to get away from him, but she knew it wasn't that easy. She wiped her nose on her sleeve. All the things they'd shared—things they did—illegal things—whether or not she liked it—there was a bond. A horrible bond. They'd been through a lot together. And she was afraid. *He'll come after me. He'll hunt me down. He'll probably kill me.*

The other voice chimed in: *He's killing you now—a slow death. You can't be happy with your life.*

No—she hated her life. She deserved better.

Patty buried her face in her hands and cried. She used to be a good person—a good girl. *Now I'm nothing. A criminal. I'm dirt. I hate it. I hate myself.*

Patty was exhausted, and her body ached, and her mind was spinning so fast. She was nervous, too, because she knew this might be her only chance to get away from Roy. He was leading her to prison sooner or later—sooner most likely. She knew she deserved better. But she also knew that he'd hunt her down and never give up until he found her. And that made her nervous. Stealing his truck made her even more nervous. Everything Roy owned—though not much—was in that truck. And it was liable to break down and then he'd find her easily. He'd beat her to death on the side of the road. She couldn't figure out what to do.

Maybe she should take William's car. That way, Roy would have his truck and all of his stuff. He'd still come after her, sure, but he wouldn't be as mad and the beating might not be as severe. What she needed was the biggest head start. She should leave now. She should take William's car and leave now. That would give her several hours and put hundreds of miles between her and Roy. It just might work.

Patty quietly crept back to the great room. She hated leaving the little bathroom and that morning shower she was so looking forward to, but time was of the essence. Patty looked over at Roy, knowing she shouldn't. Focus. Focus. She would miss the "nice" Roy when he woke up, but just then her jaw throbbed as if to remind her of the other Roy. Pig. She would never miss him. There was no such thing as "nice" Roy.

William was still snoring. She assumed his car keys were in his jeans, and the slight bulge in the right pocket appeared to be keys. Slowly, softly, she moved her fingers into his pocket. Yes, these were keys. He stopped snoring and swallowed. Shit—don't wake up. She froze. He rolled over, yanking her hand with him—still half in his pocket. Patty gripped the keys and held on. His sideways movement released the keys out of his pocket, and after he had rolled over, she was left with the keys in her hand. She exhaled softly. Gripped the keys tightly so they would not jangle.

Patty walked through the door—outside now—and shut it quietly.

Moments later, the Ford crawled down the gravel road; the taillights disappearing amongst the trees.

THREE

Miles away on the interstate, Patty had been making good time and putting many miles between her and Roy. The early morning sunrise was shining in her eyes via the rearview mirror and it was making it harder for her to keep her eyes open. Fatigue was setting in. More than once, she had to catch herself dozing off as her head bobbed down. She'd shake her head, slap her sore cheek, and continue on. William's car drove easily enough, and the radio worked fine, but Patty could swear she was now hearing the engine knock, although it sounded like it was coming from the rear of the car and not from the engine compartment.

An old song came on the radio—a song from her faraway past when she was a little girl. Monster Dad—"daddy" back then—used to turn it up whenever it came on—singing along with it at the top of his lungs about "his little girl." Sure wish time could stand still—especially if one could pick the specific time that stands still—but that wasn't the case, and one was left only with the memories—some good and most not so good. She sang along with the final refrain, and then the song ended.

It was in that moment, right after the song ended and the next radio advertisement came on, that Patty swore she heard a muffled "Help!" followed by three quick thuds—and then the radio ad blasted on. She turned the radio off and listened intently.

She knew she heard it now, and it was coming from the rear of the car. It sounded as if somebody was yelling from the trunk. Patty looked ahead and saw an exit ramp just down the road, and there was a gas station to the right of the exit.

"Hold on!" she yelled over my shoulder. "I'm going to pull over in a second!" Patty had to admit that it felt kind of strange yelling to somebody not there, but if her mind was playing tricks on her, so what—it wouldn't hurt to stop and check it out. Suddenly a horrible thought flashed into her mind—What if it was Roy hiding in there? It would be just like him to pull off something like that. Instantly, she was having second thoughts. The exit was coming up fast, and she needed to decide.

"Hello!" she yelled again.

"Help!" she heard, followed by two thumps. It didn't sound like Roy (or any of the fake voices of his that she knew). Patty made up her mind, and she took the exit and the car slowed. She turned into the gas station and pulled to a stop at the side of the building. She pulled the keys from the ignition and clambered to the trunk, where she paused and took a deep breath, a little worried about what she might find. Then she put the key in the lock and opened the trunk lid.

· · · ·

Patty gasped at the same time the woman in the trunk did. The woman looked barely conscious and dried blood was all over her forehead and the right cheek where her head must have laid. Her black hair was matted down where the blood obviously leaked, and there was a pool of wetness on the right side of the trunk. The woman moaned and reached out to Patty. She tried to raise herself, but fell back against the strain.

Patty reached in to assist her. "Here, let me help you out." She took a hold of the woman's hand and then paused. "Maybe you should stay there until I call nine-one-one. It might be better for you to stay lying down."

The woman squeezed her hand and tried to pull again. "Get me out of this god-forsaken trunk right now." The woman spoke in one breath and then gulped in a mouthful of fresh air.

"Sure, sure," Patty said. "You can rest in the back seat."

Together, they struggled to get her out of the trunk. When the woman's feet hit the pavement, she stopped to rest. "This is good for now," she said. "Thanks."

Patty didn't quite know what to do or say. She looked around—looked toward the gas station, down at the ground—she tried not to stare at the woman or her injury. "You sure you don't want to sit down in the back seat?"

The woman shook her head. "In a minute." She took a couple of deep breaths. "Who the hell are you, anyway?"

"My name is Patty." She wanted nothing more than to help this poor woman, but she had to be careful. She couldn't just call the police. After all, she had just stolen the car, complete with a battered woman in need of help in the trunk. Maybe she could get the woman inside the gas station, call nine-one-one and then make a quick getaway. But Patty figured the cops would be on her within the hour. No—that wouldn't work.

"What are you doing in my car? What am I doing in the trunk of my car?"

Did she hear the woman correctly? Did she say, "What are you doing in my car?" So did William steal it, too? Patty needed more info before she decided on her next move, but she needed to think quickly. She couldn't admit to stealing the car. "Um, a man named William said I could borrow it."

"William is my..." The woman couldn't finish the sentence. She put her head down and took more calculated breaths. "My head hurts..."

She gave the woman a few moments to gather herself. She couldn't tell which of them was more confused. Finally, when the woman seemed somewhat more composed, Patty asked, "What's your name, missus?"

"Maggie. William is my husband." Maggie put her hand to her forehead. "Where is William?"

Patty needed the Q and A to go in the opposite direction. "He's back at the cabin. How did you end up in the trunk?"

"I don't know. I only woke up a little while ago and I had no idea where I was. All I knew..." Here the woman paused again. Clearly, she was in need of help—but Patty was in need of more info. "All I know was that it was dark and my head throbbed something fierce. The whole place was rumbling, and when I tried to get up, I conked my head on the trunk lid. Almost blacked out again. I think William hit me with something, but that can't be right." She looked at Patty. "Can you get me something to drink?"

Patty nodded. "Sure, sure. I'll call nine-one-one, too." The woman moved toward the back of the car. Patty opened the back door for her and helped her in, and then she headed toward the gas station. She was so confused. Did William smack this Maggie woman—his wife— and then dump her in the trunk? It just made little sense. But how could she explain to this woman, or more importantly, to the cops, the fact that she was three hours away from the cabin, and in William's car? Could she say William and Roy were going to catch up with her later? That was an awful weak alibi. How about the discovery of Maggie and she then took off to get them both away from Roy and William—as far away and as quickly as possible? That was better, but still pretty thin. How many hospitals and sheriff's offices had she passed up all ready? Probably a lot, but it's the best she could think up at the moment.

Patty went into the gas station. The female attendant had been watching out the window, and when she entered, the girl's eyes narrowed as she sized Patty up. Patty noticed she was young, brunette, and bored. The thin, tight T-shirt the attendant wore—and how she filled it—was probably popular with the local boys. Patty's and Maggie's real-life story unfolding outside her window was better than the morning TV blasting away on the monitor behind her. She could tell the girl was highly suspicious and had a zillion questions, and Patty figured if they got the police and ambulance involved, most of the questions would be answered. "I need to call nine-one-one, please," Patty said. "There's a woman who needs help."

The girl nodded and went to the phone. She listened while the girl called and began with the details, all the while looking around the store at all the bottled waters—with all their high-price tags on them. Patty had only taken twenty dollars from Roy, and that was mainly for gas and who-knew-what—but bottled water was not high on her list of essentials. She grabbed a super-duper large cup and filled it with ice and water from the beverage machine. She then grabbed a couple of paper towels and filled these with ice—for the poor woman's head. Maybe the girl would take pity and not charge her for anything. She heard the girl finish with the nine-one-one call and hang up.

"They should be here in twenty minutes or so," the girl said. "They come from Beaumont Valley, and it's not too far."

"I just got some ice and water here. It should help with her head." Patty held them up, and the girl made no sign she wanted any money for them, so Patty didn't press her luck and bring it up herself. "OK, thanks," she said to the girl. "I'm going back out with Maggie."

She stepped back outside and felt the morning sun on her face and smelled the scent of the interstate—concrete, asphalt, exhaust fumes, smells she was all too familiar with. The woman was sitting fully in the backseat now. She handed Maggie the cup of water.

Maggie nodded and said, "Oh good—super size." She took a series of small swallows that drained half the cup, then stopped and took a deep breath. "Thank you," she said.

Patty handed her the ice pack. "Here. Put this on your head." She felt sorry for this woman. She thought she had it bad with Roy—and she did—but at least when he beat her, she remained conscious and was allowed to ride in the cab. Patty knew she'd have to come clean with this woman and tell her the truth. Maybe Maggie (and the cops) would take pity and not throw the book at her. She did steal the car, but the rationale was along the lines of self-defense and escape—that had to count for something. Patty told this woman the whole story, beginning with the pizza parlor hold-up, and how she was forced to be an accomplice. She told her how Roy had pulled a gun on William and forced him to let them stay. She told her how Roy proceeded to get very drunk and violent once again, and how William had actually stood up for her. And she told her how she got away by taking his car. "I didn't really give it too much thought except that Roy would kill me if I took his truck and I didn't think William would."

The woman had sat expressionless as she listened. "Now maybe you know different, being he tried to kill me." She paused. "William's been under a lot of pressure..."

The sound of sirens could now be heard, and they were quickly getting louder.

"I am so sorry I took your car." Patty fought the tears forming in my eyes. "I had to get away." The woman remained expressionless. "Please don't turn me in," she said.

The sheriff's car—siren wailing—came screaming into the gas station—followed closely behind by an ambulance. They both quickly came to a halt next to William's car. The sirens slowly quieted to a moan—then silence. The lights continued to flash around and around, casting strange shadows in the cloud of dust formed by the fast braking of the vehicles.

"Hello, ladies." It was the deputy, his eyes darting about—taking in the scene immediately, efficiently, professionally—suspiciously. "Can someone tell me what's going on?"

Patty couldn't look up. "She's been hurt bad. It's her head. She got hit with something, or fell and bumped her head. I'm not sure—except she's really hurt and there's blood everywhere."

The deputy motioned for the two paramedics, one male and one female, to take a look. He stood off to the side, glancing into the trunk, and then peering into the car before coming back around to the trunk. As the paramedics examined Maggie's head, Patty moved a couple of steps away and tried not to watch the deputy examine the trunk. The female paramedic said something to her male cohort, and they retrieved a stretcher from the ambulance.

As they put Maggie onto the stretcher, she said, "Officer—this is my car. She's with me." The female paramedic put a finger to her lips to indicate silence. "My husband hit me with a paddle. She helped me escape..." Maggie then moaned and put her head down.

"You need to stay quiet, please," the paramedic reaffirmed.

The deputy went back to his car and Patty saw him get on his radio. He stared back at her and she looked away to watch the paramedics load Maggie into the back of the ambulance. Another patrol car pulled up and a second deputy—maybe the sheriff—got out and went to the first officer. He was bigger and older than the first officer, and his outfit included the typical mirror aviator sunglasses. They talked briefly, and then conferred with the paramedics. They looked again at Patty, and then the second officer motioned toward the gas pumps. He came over to her.

"Hello, miss," he said. "I'm Sheriff Monroe. We got two things that we need to get done here. One is to get you and Mrs. Lancaster's statement—that's who the car checks out to—William and Margaret Lancaster—is that correct?"

She nodded hesitantly.

"OK," Sheriff Monroe said. "But the first and most important thing is to get Mrs. Lancaster to Grace Hospital. I take it you want to join her?"

Another small nod from her.

"Right," he said, pointing again at the pumps. "We'll fill the car up..." Patty moved her hand to her pocket. "This one's on the county. We'll fill 'er up and you can follow behind the ambulance in her car. We'll be right behind you. Sound good?"

"Yes, sir," Patty said—realizing the main reason was the fact that they would not let her get too far away from them. The deputy shut the trunk, and he got into William's car. He pulled it to the pump and began to fill the tank.

Sheriff Monroe cocked his head at Patty. "You OK? You haven't been hurt, too, have you?"

She tried her hardest to look at the sheriff. "Well, I was hit in the jaw, but it's OK." Her eyes looked away again.

Sheriff Monroe looked over the top of his sunglasses to examine her jaw more closely. "You sure you don't want the medics to have a look?"

Patty shook her head quickly. "No, sir. I'm OK. Thanks for your help."

"OK then. Looks like Deputy Hardy is finished. Why don't you get into the car and we'll get this parade on the road. Be sure to keep up with the paramedics."

Patty nodded one more time and did what she was told.

The ambulance pulled back onto the interstate—lights flashing and siren wailing again. She followed it while the two patrol cars kept close behind her—their lights flashing, but the sirens were at least silent—and Patty began worrying about her future again.

FOUR

The first time Roy awoke, briefly, out of his drunken stupor, he could barely open his eyes. Lead weights were attached to his lower eyelids and the upper lids were glued to the bottom ones. A sledgehammer was pounding upside his head. And so he closed his eyes again and fell back into the world of the unconscious. The second time he awoke, an hour later, he realized something was wrong. It was too quiet. *What the hell was going on? And where the hell was Patty?*

"Patty," he groaned, but it was barely audible and completely incomprehensible. "Patty!" This second groan was not much better. He stretched out, but that accomplished nothing but making his head spin and rock, and then his knee slammed into the wall and that hurt like hell.

Roy closed his eyes and took a deep breath, waiting for the pain to fade from his head and knee, which did not happen either. He could hear the heavy breathing from across the room—this would be Willy Boy. The problem, as he saw it, was that no one else was in the room. Her ropes lay unattended on the floor. Where the hell was Patty? "Patty!" he said again. "Patty!" But still no reply. Maybe she was outside. Why the hell would she be outside? Maybe she was in the bathroom. But Roy couldn't hear any water running and he could see the door open. As soon as he got a hold of that bitch, he was going to have to teach her a lesson—and teach it to her good and hard. "Patty!" Still no answer. She was only making this harder—and more painful— on herself. Yeah, Roy knew he had apologized the last time (and the time before that... and the time before that...) and he had said it would be the last time—but hell, she was supposed to change, too. She was supposed to be there for him, and to be around when he needed her. Like *now*!

Last night he'd gotten out of control—it was bad, he knew. He had hit her harder than he had meant to, but he couldn't help it. He'd been way too drunk. And the same earlier that week. She had really pissed him off then, too. The stupid truck was the real trouble. If it wouldn't have broken down, he wouldn't have had to work on it so late that night, and she wouldn't have screwed up when he told her to turn the key. And she leaned on the horn instead—blasting the fuck out of his eardrums. Louder than hell with his head under the hood! Causing Roy then to drop the flashlight. Shit—all hell broke loose, and he grabbed her out of the truck and threw her down on the ground and, well, he kind of lost control. He got sorry and apologized afterwards— made up as best he could—because he *did* feel bad about it. Shit—he knew that didn't help with the bruising and everything, but at least he said he wouldn't do it again. And he had meant it. But hell, she had pulled a gun on him last night. His gun! She had to know she was messing up! She had to know that he would lose it and straighten her ass out. It was her fucking fault!

Roy stood up. His head rocked and exploded and reminded him just how much booze he actually drank the night before. Roy leaned on the table with his right hand to steady himself and the world. "Patty," he said one more time, and one more time, he heard nothing in response. Where the hell was that girl? He looked in the bathroom— nothing. He looked in the bedroom—empty.

Roy was out of rooms to look in. Was she outside? He went to the window and peered out. Nothing. In fact, William's car was gone. What'd she do? Run to the store for milk and donuts? Surely she didn't run off. He'd fucking kill her if she did.

Roy grabbed the pistol lying on the kitchen table and marched over to the man hog-tied on the floor. He shoved the gun in William's face and flicked his nose with the barrel to wake him up.

"Wake up, asshole."

The snoring stopped, and William stirred.

William felt something cold on his nose, moving to his cheek. He tried to brush at it, but he couldn't move, and it didn't go away.

"I said wake up."

He opened one eye. It was that punk-ass Roy, and he held the gun to William's cheek.

"Where's my girl?" His breath was rancid. "Where's Patty!"

"I don't know. I guess she's gone."

Roy kicked at the table. He pulled a knife from the bar and slashed at William's ropes. With his terrible hangover and unsteady hands, it was lucky he didn't cut any flesh. William watched nervously as he cut. He was glad Roy was cutting the rope, but not too sure a slashed wrist was what he wanted, either. Roy actually made quick work of it, and after the ropes fell to the floor, William rubbed his wrists.

"Get up now! We're going after her!" He yanked William by his shirt—pulling him up. "Let's go!"

William got up and rubbed his head. He casually walked to the sink and splashed some water on his face. It was very cold, and it felt wonderful.

"You ought to try this sometimes, Roy. It's called washing."

Roy grabbed him by the T-shirt again and flung him towards the door. William crashed to the floor, and the paddle fell over. He eyed it momentarily with thoughts of grabbing it, but Roy didn't give him time to pick it up, because he kicked him toward the door. Then Roy paused for a second and leaned on the wall. William thought maybe— because he was turning a shade of green—that Roy was going to get sick. And Roy was probably thinking this, too. But whatever ailed him, he got over it quickly, and it passed. He still looked a bit ill, rather pallid, but he made sure the gun remained pointed at William. And he kept shaking his head. "I can't believe she'd up and leave me like that. Why'd she do that, anyway? Hell, she can't make it on her own. She needs me." Then all of a sudden rage filled his head, and he shoved William again. "She better not go to the police. I'll kill her if she does. She better not." Then he shook his head once again. "What she go and leave for?" He glared at William. "You talk some shit to her?"

William sat down in a chair at the table and shook his head.

"You did, didn't you?" Roy screamed. "You talked her into it. You asshole! What'd you tell her?" He stood over William, shaking the gun in his direction.

William shook his head.

"It's all your fault. Everything was fine until you came along. Then all of a sudden she gets mad—upset—with crazy thoughts in her head, and leaves me. What'd you say to her? Did you mess with her? You did, didn't you?" He was fuming again. He cocked the gun.

"Easy, Roy. That thing could go off."

"You better fucking believe it. What did you do to my Patty!"

"Look—you tied me up. Knocked me out. How could I do anything?"

"You're full of shit. You gave her your car and told her to ditch me."

William looked at Roy—adrenaline awakening inside him. "What are you talking about?"

"Don't give me that. Your car's gone and so is Patty."

William jumped up. He didn't even worry about Roy and his gun. And when he moved to the window, Roy followed behind. And Roy was right—for once. The spot where William's Ford had been parked was vacant and yawned back at them, and the rusty pickup sat alone in the drive—the midmorning sun highlighting its dust. That's just great.

"Believe me, I wouldn't give her my car in trade for your flunky truck." William saw a flash of reflected light past the truck and in the trees beyond. "Did you see that?" he asked.

"What're you talking about?"

"Something in the trees..."

Roy pushed him to the side so he could look outside. And then he saw it, too. "It's the cops." He ducked from the window. "Get down, you idiot!"

Out of kneejerk reaction, William did. And then he thought—what is this? It felt like he was living in a Butch Cassidy and the Sundance Kid movie.

"What the hell are the cops doing here? Did Patty get caught? Did she turn me in?" Roy slammed his fist into the wall. "I'll fuckin' kill her if she did."

William was sitting with his back to the wall (like Butch Cassidy)—thinking. Did Patty get caught? Did they find Maggie? Without really realizing it, he said, "I'm not sure if they're here for you... or me."

Roy was scanning the countryside for further movement, but he paused and looked down at him. "What do you mean?"

William looked at him and then figured, what the hell does it matter if he knows? Roy couldn't turn him in. "Yesterday—I basically lost it." William nodded toward the paddle. "My wife was here with me. She was driving me up the wall, so I beat her head in with that paddle. Then I dumped her in the trunk of my Ford. I assume Patty took off with her still in the trunk this morning. Maybe she found Maggie's body and turned me in."

Roy immediately busted out laughing. And he laughed for a long while, finally stopping and saying, "I don't know what's funnier: you losing your dead wife, or the look on Patty's face when she opens the trunk."

Roy's laughing bugged the hell out of William. What the hell did this asshole really understand? He was nothing but a dumbass. "Well, maybe she didn't open the trunk, Roy, and the cops are here to haul your ass back to prison."

He stopped laughing. "I'm not going back in. Never." He looked back out the window. "No fucking way I'm going back. You ever been to prison?"

"I can't say that I have."

"You wouldn't believe the things they do to you."

"Pretty rough, huh?"

"Shit—the guards—and the other prisoners mainly. I'm not being 'RoyBoy' ever again." Now it was William's turn to chuckle. Roy glared at him once and said, "Shut the fuck up!" He was ready to slam William's face with the pistol. Then, in one motion, he saw movement outside and fired through the glass. The dual sounds of the pistol booming and the shattering glass were deafening. By instinct, William dove away from the window as Roy yelled, "Get outta here, cops! I'll kill you!"

William pulled himself up off the floor and leaned against the wall. "That's making friends."

From outside they heard a voice: "We have the place surrounded!" and then a slight pause. "Maggie and Patty told us everything, and the two of you are not getting away! Come out with your hands up!"

William's dumbfounded and quizzical look on his face spoke volumes. "Did he say Maggie?"

Roy sneered. "He did. I guess she's not dead, you fuck-up. Did you make *sure* she was dead?"

William shrugged. "Well, she wasn't moving… and then you guys pulled up."

Roy shook his head and laughed. "You're a fucking idiot. You should've popped her." He made a motion with the gun. "That's what I would of done." Then he saw movement again outside, and the pistol boomed once more. "I'm tellin' you, they ain't taking me alive. I'm getting to my truck one way or another. You with me or not?"

William just looked at Roy, and then said, "Well, I'm not hitching a free ride from the cops."

"Good." Roy motioned to the back window. "Look out back and see if you eyeball more cops. They could be lying. Cops are good for that, believe me."

William did as he was instructed and went to the back window. He saw nothing but trees and brush, and with no wind, he couldn't see any movement at all—but that didn't necessarily mean there weren't any cops out there.

"Anything?" Roy asked.

"I see nothing."

"Good. If we can get them to go around back, then we'll have a clear shot out the front toward the truck… if it'll start." He motioned back toward the front. "Come back here to the front and watch. I'll go back there and run out the backdoor like we're hightailing toward the woods. Watch to see if they come around back. If they do—yell at me, and then I'm blasting back through here and out the front door with you. You get in the truck and drive. I'll jump into the bed and shoot at 'em over the tailgate."

William didn't know how good a plan it was, but he had to admit, at least Roy had a plan. And it just *might* work. He moved back and sat on the floor, peering out the front window as Roy moved to the back. Using the pistol, Roy busted the back window out—doing a good job of being as noisy as possible. William saw the two cops perk up out of the brush like prairie dogs, and then the one motioned to the other. This second cop immediately started around the one side of the cabin, while the first cop started around the other side.

"I can't believe it. They're moving already," William said. "Only two of them, too. At least that's all I can see."

Roy came back to the front and sneered. "They're bigger idiots than you." He looked at William. "Are they clear?"

"Yeah, I guess so."

"Well, no better time than now. Here're the keys. It starts really hard—just keep at it and on the gas. Let's go!" And out the door he went.

William dashed behind, and they sprinted to the old pickup. Roy jumped into the bed as William opened the driver's door—it creaked and squeaked loudly—and he jumped in. When William turned the key, the engine did a slow grind, then slowed some more and almost croaked to a complete stop, until finally kicking to life at the same time that Roy fired his gun. At least William thought it was his gun. It could have been a backfire because the engine squealed loudly and then a vast cloud of smoke came pouring out of the exhaust and blanketed the area in a fog. What great cloud cover.

"Get going!" Roy yelled.

William jammed the truck into gear and blasted down the driveway, spitting gravel and dirt behind them as they went. This time, he heard what he *knew* were a couple of shots, but they were coming *their* way. It was the first time he'd ever been shot at, and he didn't like it one bit. He ducked down into the seat as the truck bounced and rocked down the road.

He heard Roy rapping on the back window. "Pull over and let me in."

They bounced to a stop, and instantly Roy was opening the passenger's door. "Wait here," he said, and he ran away from the truck and off down the road a ways. William saw beyond him the squad car. Two reports from Roy's gun meant the tires were shot out. Another shot was most likely their radio. Roy came back to the truck, but just before he got in, he turned back toward the squad car and fired once more. The emergency lights on the roof shattered. He jumped in the truck. "Just for good measure, you know." He laughed. And then all of a sudden he was in a hurry again. "Come on! Let's go!"

They made their way down the gravel road and came to the intersection at the county road. Which way to turn was the million-dollar question. William looked at Roy for direction. "Which way, boss?"

Roy looked back at William. "Hell, I don't know. Go this way," and he motioned to the left. William turned that way and the pavement felt good under the tires.

"We gotta find Patty," Roy said. "You got a cellphone, don't ya?"

William nodded.

"Well, call 'em up."

William shook his head. "I haven't had a signal since we left the last little town. Besides, I don't think Maggie really wants to talk to me... or tell me where she is."

"It's worth a shot."

William looked at Roy, and a thought hit him. "You know, we do have a phone app that has GPS tracking. I've never tried it, but... One: her phone battery has to be alive. Two: she has to have it on. Three: I have to figure out how to tap into it."

"Well, hell. Try it."

"I need a signal first."

"Shit." Roy nodded ahead. "I think there's a town further up. Track 'em there."

"That's assuming Patty's with her, too."

"She's with her. Patty can't do nothing on her own." He looked at Roy. "She left your sorry ass."

Roy flushed the gun at William's face. "You know, why don't I just put you out of my fucking misery."

"How are you going to find Patty, then?" William asked.

Roy glared at him, then he slowly dropped the gun. "Just drive, ass wipe."

As they made their way down the road, William wondered how the hell he had ended up in this miserable mess? It was only a couple of days ago when he was living comfortably—well, maybe not comfortably, but at least normally—with a wife and a house and at least a simple life. And now here he was on the run with a two-bit criminal low-life character whom he didn't know at all and liked even less. And with murder (or attempted murder?) hanging over him. Add to that resisting arrest and who knows what else he was linked to as an accomplice, because he was mixed up with this loser. One bad choice at one bad moment and look where it landed him. Mama always told him to just make the right decisions and everything would work out. Man—to only be able to turn back the clock.

They arrived at the outskirts of town, and William checked his cell phone. He had reception again.

Roy pointed up ahead. "See that pizza joint? Pull in there."

William pulled into the parking lot, but stayed at the far end so as not to attract attention. Another car pulled into the parking lot and stopped at the front door. William noticed a shaggy-haired guy in blue jeans jump out and unlocked the front door of the joint. The man casually inspected the front of the store and the surrounding area, and then picked up a piece of paper trash he noticed on the ground. He crammed the paper into his pocket before hopping back into his car and heading for the rear of the building through the alleyway.

As the car went past, Roy spotted him. "Well, if it isn't pizza owner beatnik dude." Roy laughed. "Come on. This'll be fun."

He jumped out and headed toward the back of the building where the car had just disappeared. William followed behind, and when they turned the corner, they saw the beatnik-looking dude just entering through the back door. Roy raced over and caught the pizza place door just before it shut, and he ducked inside.

The owner heard them and turned around to face them. "We are not open yet," he said, and then got this pained look on his face—like he had terrible gas—as he recognized Roy. "Oh, you gotta be kiddin' me."

Roy grinned and pulled his gun out of his pants. He pointed it at the owner. "I take it you remember my pretty face."

The pizza owner raised his hands—ala Butch Cassidy and the Sundance Kid. "Look—I don't have any money. You took it all yesterday."

Roy laughed. "Oh, but I ran out. You gotta have a little more."

"I haven't even opened yet. I got like a handful of ones—that's all."

Roy waved him backward and out of the kitchen area into the front parlor. "We'll take 'em." The owner dude went to the register and Roy turned to William. "Do your GPS-thing, or whatever it's called, Willy Boy. We ain't got all day."

William went to one of the tables, sat down, and pulled out his phone to see if he could locate Maggie. He heard the cash register open.

"Well, lookie there," Roy said. "You got some cash in there. And you know what? Check your wallet, too. I bet there's some in there, too." The guy pulled out his wallet and gave Roy his cash. Roy pocketed it all, then he picked up the pizza parlor telephone. "You got a new one fast."

The pizza dude shrugged. "A pizza place gotta have a phone — only way to make money."

"Good thing, too — otherwise you might have been broke this morning. We wouldn't want that, would we?" Roy yanked on the phone cable. It held tight, and he yanked harder. It finally came busting through the drywall — flakes scattering everywhere.

The pizza owner winced. "Aw, come on, man," he said. "I just had that fixed."

Roy pointed the gun at the guy's head. "Shut the fuck up — and move back to the kitchen." The pizza owner walked slowly to the back area, hands up again. Roy kept the pistol trained on the back of pizza dude's head as his shit-ass grin reappeared. He was obviously in his element: two-bit armed robbery. Roy glanced around. "You got any rope back here?"

The pizza owner shook his head, but just then Roy spotted the leftover spool of telephone wire from yesterday's new install in the corner. "Ah — this'll work," he said. He motioned downward with the pistol. "Sit."

The guy sat down on the floor amongst all the dirt and grim and pizza sauce. Roy tied his hands and legs to the side of a large metal rack filled with pizza sauce cans: big cans and small cans, "mild sauce" cans and "fire sauce" cans, brand new sealed cans and some that had been used and left opened. "Now don't start fidgeting. You might knock all that sauce over on top of your little head. That would hurt." He brushed an open can with his elbow on purpose. It fell over and hit the pizza guy on the head, splattering pizza sauce all over him. The guy grimaced, and Roy laughed. "See—hurts, doesn't it? And we can't waste that special sauce now, either, can we? That your special sauce?"

The guy just shook his head, trying not to show the pain that was obvious from the falling can and the goose egg forming on the top of his forehead. "Why are you picking on me?" His eyes were actually watering.

Roy laughed again and finished up his knot. "Maybe I like you. But you know, we have to quit meeting like this—people will begin to talk." Again the goofy laugh from comedian Roy. He noticed a roll of large tape on the shelf and peeled off a piece. He stuck it to the pizza dude's face, covering his mouth, then he came back out front and grabbed the keys that the pizza guy had left on the counter. "Find anything out, Willy Boy? We gotta go."

William had to smile. He *was* able to track a location. "You will not believe this, but I found them. They appear to be at a hospital in Beaumont Valley, Missouri. Bad thing is they have a seven-hour head start on us."

"Good job, Willie Boy. I'm impressed." He tossed William the keys. "We got ourselves a new car now. Let's get the hell out of here before the cops show up."

PART FOUR

ONE

The two cops had found their patrol car in a shambles. With two flat tires and a shot out radio, they were forced to walk until they would be able to access cell reception. Fortunately for them, a local passed by, and they could catch a ride after only walking a couple of miles. As they piled into JD Warren's station wagon, he nodded at them in greeting.

"Y'all having car trouble?" JD asked.

"Yeah, JD," Officer Blakey said, getting in and riding shotgun.

Officer Downey tried to find room to sit in the back seat amongst all the crap that JD had in the car. Car parts, plant boxes, tools, clay pots, magazines, spent shotgun shells, and various items of clothing littered the back seat and the cargo area in the rear.

"Damn, JD," Officer Downey said, "ever think about cleaning this mess?"

JD grinned. "You never know when you might need something, you know?"

Officer Blakey kept his eye on his cell phone reception as he reflected on their morning's tactical maneuvers. "OK, so that didn't work out too good. We need to learn from this. We should have split up—one of us in the front of the house and one of us going to the back."

"Well, hell, we couldn't know. We should have had more back up," Officer Downey said. "And that wasn't our fault." He shook his head.

"True, but time was of the essence."

"So what these guys do? Serial killers?" JD asked.

"One of them is a two-bit robber. He robbed Amici's Pizza yesterday. Probably robbed a whole slew of mom and pop joints across the state. They caught his girlfriend in Beaumont Valley."

"The other guy tried to kill his wife with a paddle. How they ended up together—well, it's pretty convoluted."

"Hey, it's ringing," Officer Blakey said, glad he finally had enough reception to get through. "Yeah, this is Officer Blakey." He put out an alert on Roy's old truck. As he was talking, the station wagon made its way into town, and he noticed the pickup in the parking lot of Amici's Pizza. "There's that damn truck now!" He pointed ahead. "OK, pull down past the place and we'll sneak back up on it." He looked at Officer Downey. "Don't look. They might still be in the place—or somewhere around it."

The car pulled off into Reed's Service Station. The two cops jumped out. "Thanks, JD," Officer Blakey said. "We'll catch you later. We gotta catch ourselves some bad guys." He shut the door and the station wagon pulled slowly away.

"Man, he has a lot of crap in that car," Officer Downey said, brushing down his uniform.

"Come on. Draw your gun. Let's go get these guys." The two officers snuck down the row of businesses and then ducked into the alley next to the pizza parlor. It was quiet, and they were alone. Officer Blakey nudged Officer Downey. "Go make sure no one is in the truck." Officer Downey looked at him with concern. "Don't worry. I'll back you up. From right here," he said, as he leaned up against the corner of the building.

Officer Downey hesitated nervously, and with good reason; after all, he could easily get plugged. He ran up to the back of the truck and squatted low. Then he ever so slowly peered over the bed with his pistol at the ready. Nothing. He looked back at Officer Blakey and shook his head while he mouthed the words "nothing." Then he held up one finger and moved slowly down the side of the truck, but still keeping low. At the passenger door, he jumped up and pointed his gun inside, while saying, "Freeze!"

At the corner, Officer Blakey flinched momentarily, and then waited to see the outcome. But nothing happened once again.

The two officers straightened simultaneously, and then Officer Downey shrugged. Officer Blakey waved at him to come back to the corner. "They must still be inside Amici's. I can't believe they came back to Homer's restaurant. Cover me. I'm going to the front door."

Officer Blakey crept softly to the door, his pistol drawn, his nerves on high alert. He peeked into the window and saw nothing unusual. He could see through the restaurant and there was a light on in the back—but that could be a normal thing—Homer maybe leaves a light on all night. His car wasn't out front, but he probably parked in the rear, anyway. Damn—should have noted that first. Oh well, time to try the door.

He gripped the doorknob ever so softly and turned. It turned with him. That was good—it was unlocked. He looked once more in the window and when he still saw nothing out of place, he motioned for Officer Downey to join him. He didn't want to have all the fun—or danger. Officer Downey moved silently, quickly to Officer Blakey's side, his pistol drawn, too.

Officer Blakey softly pushed the door open—hoping that the hinges did not squeak. It was silent. Thank God.

About halfway open—the little bell they had forgotten about that hung over the door to let everyone know if someone comes in—well, it dropped and released a ding-a-ling loudly—announcing the two ding-a-ling cops' entrance. In the second that followed, Officer Blakey said, "Shit!" and dove to his left behind a table. Officer Downey dove to the right and landed behind a second table. They both whipped back up, raising their guns, and pointing toward the back. The reverberation from the bell slowly faded away, and the room became deathly silent.

They waited another second, and then when nothing changed, Officer Blakey looked at Officer Downey, and then he dove forward, landing at the base of the counter. He rose again with his gun pointed to the back while Officer Downey moved up to his side. They waited—listening.

"Mmm." The sound was faint, but it was there—coming from the back. "Mmm." A little louder this time. Officer Blakey quickly moved to the back room entrance, and after Officer Downey came up behind him, he burst into the back room with his pistol raised.

The body just inside the room tripped him up, and he went sprawling. Officer Blakey's gun went off as Officer Downey went down and landed on top of him. The bullet hit the fire extinguisher hanging on the wall, and it immediately began hissing out a spray of chemicals. It was Homer, lying on the floor—tied up and with tape covering his mouth.

Officer Blakey jumped up and his eyes darted around, thankful his gunshot appeared to have been harmless—other than the hissing fire extinguisher. "Anyone else here?" he asked.

"Mmm," was all Homer said. Officer Blakey reached over and with one quick motion ripped the packing tape off of his mouth. Homer let out a scream of pain.

"Oh, sorry, Homer," he said. "You OK? Anybody here?"

Homer, with his eyes squinched closed and in pain, licked his lips. "Damn, Orville, you ripped my lips off."

"Sorry, sorry, man. I'm a little pumped."

"Nobody is here," Homer said. "They took off in my car about an hour ago. Could you untie me, please—and get off me, Rickey!"

Officer Downey got up while Officer Blakey found a knife and cut Homer free. He was covered in gooey pizza sauce. Officer Blakey swiped a dollop of sauce from his shoulder with his finger and licked it off. "Good sauce, Homer, but you're a mess."

"No shit. Not having a good day—a good week." Officer Downey swiped some sauce off of Homer as he got up and tasted it, too. Homer shook his shoulder away. "Knock it off, Rickey." Homer went to the dishwashing station and hosed himself clean as best he could.

The two cops looked at each other, and then back at Homer. Officer Blakey spoke. "Well, if you're OK, we need to go after these guys. What kind of car did you have?"

"It's a green Impala. And I'd like to get it back."

"Sure. Sure." Officer Blakey wrote down the make in his notebook, then Homer told him the license plate number and year and that it was a four-door. "I wonder where our backup is, Officer Downey? We gotta go. And no car."

"Well, their pickup is still outside," Homer said.

"Yeah, like we're going to take that." But then he realized it was better than nothing—and better than waiting around all day for the backup. Moments later, the truck backfired, slowly kicked to life, and the heavy fog from its exhaust blanketed the area. The truck backfired once again, and then Officer Blakey and Officer Downey pulled onto the road, once again in hot pursuit.

•   •   •

Patty helped Maggie into the car. "You know," she said, pulling out of the hospital parking lot, "you have been so good to me. After everything that has happened, most people would have ditched me, but you didn't, and are actually helping. Thank you."

Maggie sat with her hands in her lap. Her head—at least the top section—looked like something from an old mummy movie. It was heavily bandaged, but she was doing a lot better. "Oh, sweetie, you didn't do anything to me." The woman shook her head. "Trouble is, I can't for the life of me understand what got into William. He's been under a lot of pressure lately, but I just don't know. I thought he still loved me..." She was gazing off down the road, staring at nothing, and stayed that way for a moment or two, then she sat up straight and looked back at me. "I'm glad to help you. Besides, I can't drive, so you're helping me, too."

"I feel bad driving so far away; only to turn around and head right back in the direction we came."

"Well, we had to get away from our deadbeat husbands."

Patty shook her head quickly. "Roy will come after me. There is no way he'll let me get away. He'll come after me—probably kill me. At least beat me. And all I really want to do is try to better myself."

"Hopefully, the police have caught up with them by now."

"Oh, Roy is going to be so mad. He hates prison with a passion. They used to call him RoyBoy, and he talked about that for the longest time after he got out. You know, after he got out, he was actually pretty nice for a while."

"See—it's good for him."

"Oh, he doesn't see it that way. If they don't arrest him, he'll come after me. He'll beat me... kill me..."

"Sweetie, he'll never find us. You stay with me until we find out for sure. Then you'll connect with someone back home. We've talked about it. It's decided."

"I know, but I'm so nervous. I'm terrified—really terrified."

"Oh, don't think about it. We'll be fine." Maggie looked at her and Patty could tell she wanted to change the subject. Not sure if her idea to change the subject was the best, but it got them off subject—slightly. "How did you and Roy meet, anyway?"

"Oh, we've known each other since school. We had class together—well, at least whenever Roy decided to show up—which wasn't very often. But when he did—well, I couldn't keep my eyes off of him. And there's something about a bad boy, you know?"

Maggie said nothing. No—she probably knew nothing about "bad boys," even though her husband "went bad." He was probably the perfect guy until then. Perfect—boring. Perfectly boring.

"He had a car—not much of one—but it made it easy to go out," Patty continued, "although all we did was make out most of the time. My mom had been killed in a car crash the summer before my freshman year, and I moved in with Aunt Meredith, who was nice enough, but—well, let's just say it was easy to go unnoticed. Roy finally quit school and got a good job in construction. He got a little apartment, and I began staying more and more at his place. We were doing great for a couple of months, but then he started spending most of his money on booze. And tools started disappearing at work. Roy got blamed for it, but he said it wasn't him. He said he was framed. They didn't believe him and he lost his job. At first he started taking it out on me, and then he robbed his first gas station, and then his second, and then—somewhere along the line, his luck ran out and the cops caught him. I didn't see him for two years and had really forgotten about him. At least I'd tried. I'd actually got a little job and started going to night school, and was doing OK considering—until he showed up at my Aunt Meredith's doorstep and away we went again. Not really sure why I went, except Roy would have beaten the hell out of me if I'd refused. Well, here we are now. Same thing but a different day." She thought for a second. She'd come full circle in the conversation. "He's going to kill me."

"We'll get you back to Aunt Meredith's house—after we make sure the coast is clear. We'll go to my house first. My place will be safe. Roy won't know where it is unless William tells him. And there's no reason for William to tell him. I mean, why would you tell a low-life robber where you live, right? No offense, but Roy is what he is..."

"But how will we know when it's safe?"

"Well, we'll make some calls. Officer Wilkin gave us his card. He'll know what's up. But I'm sure the police have caught them. And I am not going to bail William out. It'll serve him right. I can't believe he hit me like that. I knew he was under a lot of stress, but come on—a paddle—that's ridiculous."

It was ridiculous indeed. The car continued on down the two-lane highway—getting closer and closer back to where it all began.

The Amici's Pizza car flew past the "Welcome to Missouri" sign. Roy let out a hoop and a holler. "We are home free!" Roy was really getting on William's nerves. Roy was one of those all-time annoying-type people: a know-it-all who was also a dumb shit. And he talked almost as much as Maggie—if that was possible. And now, after stopping at the liquor store, and Roy had a couple of beers in him, he was even worse.

"So why is crossing the state line that much better?" William asked him. "Don't the police from one state play nice with the police from another state?" He couldn't see the good men in blue from Oklahoma not alerting the ones in Missouri about a couple of felons in a stolen pizza car.

"Well, they're nice to each other," Roy said, "but the level of concern goes way down once the criminals are out of the home state. Kind of like—'their problem now,' you know? Wanna beer?"

"No, I don't want a beer. That's the last thing I need is a DUI."

Roy started laughing. God—William hated that laugh. "You are funny, Willy Boy. Like the judge will really give a shit that you are drinking a beer—as he busts you for attempted murder." He rubbed his one index finger over the index finger of the other hand. "Shame on you, Willy Boy, for drinking a beer. Ha ha ha."

Well, Roy did have a point—the little jerk—still, William wasn't thirsty. Roy was playing with the phone—probably breaking it. He was supposed to be keeping an eye on the blip that was Maggie's phone, but he tired of that a couple of hours ago and was now infatuated with the latest apps. At least it kept him quiet some of the time, unless he was making dumb jokes. Like the one as they went through the town of Beaver Dam. ("Hey, let's stop and get us some damn beaver in Beaver Dam. What you think, Willy Boy? Ha ha ha.") Just hilarious material. They did stop and get beer in Beaver Dam, though, and no, William did not want one. "Roy, check the GPS on Maggie, please."

"Willy Boy, she's in the hospital. She's not going anywhere." He started punching some buttons. "Just to make you happy and keep you off my back, I'll look." He punched more buttons. "Aw, shit, everything went away now. These phones suck." He punched more buttons. "Everything is fuckin' gone now."

William tried to see what he was doing, but no luck. "Roy, Roy, just push the bottom button." He did something. "Did that take you back home?"

"Hell, I don't know."

"Then just tap the little map symbol. That should take you right there." He pushed something else, and William at least saw something change on the display.

"Well, I don't know. The little arrow thing is not on Beaumont Valley anymore. It's over by the border now."

William shook his head. "No, no, that's us."

"Hell it is. We're here past Vinita." William grabbed the phone from his hand, causing them to swerve off the road. He yanked the wheel back, and they bounced back onto the pavement. "Damn, Willy Boy, you're going to kill us."

William tried to look and drive, but he had no idea what Roy had done to the phone, so he kept his eye out for a place to pull over. Roy grabbed the phone back out of his hand. "Hold on, Roy. Don't mess with anything. I'll pull over up here and take a look." They came upon a gravel road after a mile or so, and he pulled off. "Can I please have my phone now, Roy?"

He chucked it into William's lap. "Here—have the piece of shit. You figure it out."

William looked at the map, and it indeed showed the second blip next to the first—actually the two blips were almost one. "What the hell? According to this, they should be right here by *us*." William casually looked in the rear-view mirror—just as his Ford went past. "What the hell!" He twisted his head around, but the thick trees blocked his view down the road. William jammed the car into reverse and jumped on the gas. It might have been his imagination. He needed a better view.

Roy's beer spilled, and he said, "Shit!"

Roy's yell made William jerk to the left, and the car went into the ditch. Now William said, "Shit!"

And as the car bounced into the ditch, Roy spilled more of his beer and he said, "Shit!" again. "What the hell you doin', Willy Boy?"

"I swear I just saw Maggie go by."

"What!"

"I saw my Ford in the mirror. At least I thought I did."

"Well, let's go after 'em!"

"We're stuck."

"Shit."

"Push the car out."

"You gotta be fuckin' kiddin' me?" Roy said as he got out of the car.

• • •

Roy's old beat up truck was parked on the shoulder of the two-lane highway. Officer Blakey and Officer Downey were standing outside of it, and although it was a beautiful day, they were not enjoying the weather. As Officer Blakey talked to headquarters about their next move, he stared ahead at the "Welcome to Missouri" sign. It was not a pretty sight. Officer Downey had insisted on stopping earlier and getting something to eat, and he chomped noisily on a candy bar. Officer Blakey's stomach growled and made him wish he had gotten one, too. But really, the only thing he wanted was these two-bit criminals that had terrorized his county — well, terrorized Homer anyway.

"I understand, Chief," Officer Blakey said into his cell phone, "but I don't believe they are too far ahead. I'm sure we can catch up with them soon." He listened to Headquarters holler. HQ was having none of it and was playing strictly by the book. The only time officers were allowed to cross state lines was if they were in the middle of a hot pursuit, and although the argument could be made they were in pursuit, the "hot" part about it was debatable, and headquarters didn't even want to get into the issue that they were patrolling along in the criminal's beat-up truck and not their own patrol car. And headquarters was not the *least* bit happy about the condition of their patrol car.

"OK, Chief," Officer Blakey said. "We'll hang here while you connect with the Missouri boys in case they want to stop in and see us — or perchance we have already passed up Homer's stolen car." That was unlikely. These two-bit guys always hightailed it for the state line as if that was the Promised Land (or some kind of sanctuary). Pissed Officer Blakey off.

He put the phone back on its clip as Officer Downey finished the candy bar, tossing the empty wrapper into the bed of the truck. "Kind of handy having a trash can connected to your vehicle," he said, eyeballing the garbage already littering the bed. A semi blew passed and the candy wrapper swirled in the breeze it created. Another car went by, coming from the Missouri side.

"We're supposed to hang tight," Officer Blakey replied. "What a waste. Man, we were so close…"

Officer Downey nodded, and then his eyes went wide as he pointed over Officer Blakey's shoulder toward Missouri. He said, "No way," as Officer Blakey turned to look where he pointed. A car with an Amici's Pizza sign on its roof blew past them, re-entering their wonderful state of Oklahoma.

They jumped into the old truck and it slowly, ever so slowly, grinded to a start, backfiring twice — three times — before kicking to life. The screaming noise and the plume of smoke covered them once again as they turned the vehicle around to pursue their criminals one more time.

"Come on! Step on it!" Roy yelled.

"You know, this is a pizza delivery vehicle and not built for maximum speed."

"Just catch up to 'em. Patty never drives over the speed limit—nowhere near it, actually. They got to be coming up soon."

William saw what was probably the Ford up ahead. "That looks like them."

"Well, pull up next to them. Hopefully she'll pull over so we can 'talk.'" Roy chuckled. "I got a few choice words for her—you better believe it."

They caught up to the car ahead, and it was indeed the Ford. William could see two heads in the front seat—one was bandaged up with white dressing, while the other had dirty blonde hair blowing in the wind created by the open window.

"Well, come on, pull up next to them," Roy said.

"Wait a second. I don't feel like slamming head on into the semi coming at us."

"Yeah yeah yeah. Come on."

The semi soared past them and William saw no more oncoming vehicles. It was a straight stretch, too, so he eased the pizza car into the passing lane and sped up.

The wind in Patty's hair felt good—there was a sense of freedom in the feeling. She had learned to partially tune out Maggie because the woman could talk forever and ever. And a lot of what was said was just prattle. But she was a pleasant woman, and if she wanted to talk the whole seven/eight/nine hours—that was OK with Patty.

A passing car came up on her left and honked its horn. Maggie looked beyond Patty at the car and shrieked. That made Patty jump, and she looked quickly at the car passing them—or rather not passing them, but driving beside them in the wrong lane. Her heart leapt into her throat. Roy was in the car—the passenger side—and was opening and closing his raised hand slowly in a wave—a sly grin on his face. She saw him mouth the words "Hello, Patty," as she swerved and ran off the road. She righted the car and looked back at Roy. He was now laughing, and then he motioned for them to pull over.

"What should I do, Maggie?"

Maggie looked petrified. "I can't believe they're together. I can't believe they found us. I can't believe it." She shook her head and absent-mindedly looked forward. "I can't believe it," she repeated. They honked the horn again.

"We'd better pull over," Patty said, "otherwise I'm sure he'll run us off the road."

.   .   .

Thank God the girl pulled off the road. William knew the highway had light traffic, but he was sure Roy would have made him stay in the oncoming lane even if a car came at them. He was still slamming the beers and was getting more and more fired up. So when Patty pulled off onto a little gravel road, he tee-heed like a little girl.

Then instant sarcasm and anger. "Oh, Patty, Patty," he said to the air, "so good to see you again. I've missed you so much. Have you missed me?"

He went on and on—totally oblivious to William in the same space as he was. Off in his own little world. It was somewhat disconcerting to William, to say the least, and he was worried about where it might lead them.

Patty moved on down the road a ways, and some distance ahead, the road widened for a few yards, so she pulled off to the side. William pulled up next to her and Roy was out the door before the car even stopped. Three steps in two seconds and he was ripping open Patty's door and dragging her out of the front seat. She landed hard on the gravel.

"Hello, Patty!" he said. He picked her up again and shoved her toward the front of the car. As William got out, he heard her scream.

"Stop it, Roy!" she yelled.

"It's so nice to see you, Patty. Did you miss me?"

Patty fell to the ground again as Roy slapped her hard across the face. William went toward them as they struggled on the road in front of the car. He didn't even acknowledge Maggie as she got out of her car. He wasn't sure what to do. Roy was raging, and the gun was loaded. Roy slapped Patty again when she tried to get up, which prevented her from doing so.

"Fed me to the wolves, eh?" he said. "You fuckin' bitch."

William had to say something. He had to step in, even if he might get shot. He took a step forward, but suddenly felt a slam up the side of his head. His skull exploded in pain—a bright flash—and then blackness.

.   .   .

Roy was raging. Patty lost count of how many times he had hit her. He had started with his open hand, but quickly moved to his fists. She knew it was only a short time and that pistol in his other hand would make its way to her face—not the first time he pistol-whipped her. Patty was screaming and yelling and telling him to stop—what else could she do? She noticed Maggie get out and calmly go to the back of the car. Maggie opened up the trunk and the next thing Patty saw was a crowbar in her hands. She quietly walked up behind William, who was watching Patty and Roy—and doing *nothing*—and Maggie swung that crowbar and it smashed into the side of William's head. He was out cold immediately and fell to the ground. Good for her. Roy didn't even notice.

"They could have killed me, Patty—or worse—sent to prison. How could you??!!" And then the fist again. Patty went down one more time. She knew better than to stay down. That would only mean kicking, and kicking was worse than the fists. So she started to get up again as Maggie came up behind Roy—as quiet as a mouse—and swung the crowbar towards Roy's head. He noticed the flash at just the last second and ducked his head. The crowbar glanced off the top of his head, but it sent him to the ground—sprawling.

As Maggie tried to swing again, Roy jumped up and grabbed her arm. He threw her to the ground. "You want some of this, too, bitch?"

And he was on top of her, flailing at her bandaged head. That really had to hurt.

The gun had landed next to Patty, and she picked it up and pointed it at Roy. "Stop, Roy!" As usual, he paid no attention to her. Patty pointed the gun in the air and fired. The blast was deafening and got his attention. "Stop, Roy! It's over!"

Roy stopped and stared at her. Then a smile broke out across his face and he got off of Maggie. She rolled over and grabbed her head.

"Aw, baby, baby," Roy started. "I didn't mean anything." He had instantly calmed down and was moving slowly toward Patty. "Let's kiss and make up. I promise I'll make all things better."

"Stay back, Roy. I mean it."

"Patty, honey, come on. Put the gun down." He was getting closer and closer. "I'll quit drinking for good and quit the robbing and get a real job. I know of a construction job back home. I'm ready to grow up," he said, making "grow up" quote marks with his fingers. A big smile spread across his face. "Everything will be fantastic. You'll see."

"You're not doing this to me anymore, Roy. It's finished." Over his shoulder Patty saw his old truck creeping up the road. Who was in there? Roy turned and saw it coming, too. He turned back to Patty. "Last chance, honey. This is it. Really."

Then he rushed her, saying, "I need the fuckin' gun NOW!" As his hand wrapped around the barrel, still pointing at him, it went off. Another deafening blast filled the air. Roy's eyes went wide, and he released the gun. He took a step back away from Patty and his hands went to his chest as he looked down. Blood began to pour through his fingers and down the front of his shirt. He looked back at her and — then — fell over backwards.

Two cops had gotten out of the truck and were creeping up along the two cars. Their guns were drawn. William stirred on the ground. Maggie sat up, holding her head. Roy didn't move — the red splotch growing on his shirt and seeping onto the ground. Patty dropped the gun.

So Patty got Roy's truck back. Maggie got a ride home in her car from the one officer, and William got a ride to jail by the other officer. They hauled away Roy in an ambulance—lights not shining and the siren not on. He was gone. DOA. Patty's emotions were all over the place, but one thing was for sure: he was gone from her life. She was rid of him. He would influence her life no more.

Easier said than done, but it was a start.

So Aunt Meredith took her back in and helped her start anew. She returned to her old job, started going to church, and was able to resume night classes at the local community college. She was determined to move forward and better herself. Determined. Determined. Determined. It was an everyday process.

Maggie was extremely angry with William for the longest time, but by the time his case went to court, two years had passed and her anger had somewhat died down. Besides, she was still married to him. She could have divorced (attempted murder is grounds…) but why? It's not like she was meeting anyone new or anything. When boredom set in from sitting around the house all day, she began making the trek to visit William at the penitentiary. Maggie went once or twice a week— sometimes three or four times—and could visit with him for six hours each time. He said little. He just sat and listened to her like he always had. So Maggie got to talk. And talk. And talk.

"You should see Patty these days. Well, I haven't seen her *recently*, but the last time I *did* see her was at the meeting with those movie people. Can you believe they gave Patty and me both 250 thousand dollars for our story? I can't wait to see the movie—I wonder who will play me? I hope it's somebody really pretty. Although the movie people said that most films optioned—that's the technical term for stories that are bought—they said most films optioned don't get made. That seems like a waste, doesn't it? Anyway, Patty took her money and who knows what happened to her. Good for her, I say. Good for her. That Roy guy was the worst. He was mean through and through—not like you. You just went off the deep end for a brief stretch. You know, most people think I should dump you, but why?

Who else am I going to talk to? You listen to me. You always have been a good listener. Did you know that about yourself? It's one of your best qualities. You are a good listener."

William's eyes had glazed over. He sat there across from Maggie and her ramblings just pounded into his head. But he knew it would be over soon enough. Six hours of torture—listening to her—and then they would take him back to his cell, where it was quiet and peaceful once again.

It was quiet and peaceful on the beach where the young lady sat and sipped her drink with the little umbrella on the top. She stared out far away to the deep blue waters and listened to the waves as they lapped at the shore. She was collecting her thoughts, her pen in her hand, her notebook on her lap. The little butterfly tattoo that peaked out above her bikini bottom was finally flying free.

Acknowledgments

Considered by many to be an isolated process, this is never the case when writing a novel. Many people have helped me with the creation of this story and I want to thank them here. My apologies to anyone I might have inadvertently forgotten.

This story was born of a short story for a Fiction Writing class. Thanks to everyone in that class from Meramec Community College who gave me feedback, and our teacher Kristen. This story also became a Senior Portfolio project for me at Webster University, and could not have been done without the help of James Arand, Lois Giles, Paul Luckritz, and Michelle Ridgly. This also included Tim Dixon, Jon Broyles, Cindy Morley, Brad Morley, Steve Luckritz, Paesono's Pizza, Gloria Langewisch, Hope Lutheran church, and now I know I am forgetting people.

Thanks also to my early readers Michelle Farmer, David Fiedler, Jan Edwards, and to my later readers Sam Kaeding, David Schmitt and Stephen Briggs.

Thanks to my publisher Reagan Rothe for giving me this chance.

Thank you to my wonderful wife Suzanne for always being there.

And thanks to you, the readers, who, without you, none of this would matter!

ABOUT THE AUTHOR

During the day Dale Ward is an award-winning filmmaker and videographer, while his night job is writer, reader and family man. Films he has written include *My Life Is a Movie, Walther, Ragman* (with appearances in more than 50 film festivals), and *There's Something in the Basement*. He has won 4 regional Emmy awards producing the national television talk show *On Main Street*, and he earned a Bachelor of Arts in Media Communications from Webster University. His publishing history includes *The Home Run, Delayed Reactions*, and *My Life Is a Movie*. He makes his home in St. Louis, Missouri with his wife, Suzanne, and two sons

NOTE FROM THE AUTHOR

Word-of-mouth is crucial for any author to succeed. If you enjoyed *Killing the Butterfly*, please leave a review online — anywhere you are able. Even if it's just a sentence or two. It would make all the difference and would be very much appreciated.

Thanks!
Dale Ward